S0-EAU-449

TALENT NIGHT

Congratulations
on your award!

Jean Davies Okimoto

Also by Jean Davies Okimoto

PLAYS
Hum It Again, Jeremy
Uncle Hideki
Uncle Hideki and the Empty Nest

NOVEL
The Love Ceiling

NONFICTION
Boomerang Kids: How to Live with Adult Children Who Return Home (coauthor)

YOUNG ADULT NOVELS
My Mother Is Not Married to My Father
It's Just Too Much
Norman Schnurman, Average Person
Who Did It, Jenny Lake?
Jason's Women
Molly by Any Other Name
Take a Chance, Gramps!
Talent Night
The Eclipse of Moonbeam Dawson
To JayKae: Life Stinx
Maya and the Cotton Candy Boy

PICTURE BOOKS
Blumpoe the Grumpoe Meets Arnold the Cat
A Place for Grace
No Dear, Not Here
Dear Ichiro
The White Swan Express (coauthor)
Winston of Churchill: One Bear's Battle Against Global Warming

SHORT STORIES
"Jason the Quick And the Brave"
"Moonbeam Dawson and the Killer Bear"
"Next Month. ..Hollywood!"
"Watching Fran"
"Eva and the Mayor"
"My Favorite Chaperone"

Talent Night

Jean Davies Okimoto

ENDICOTT AND HUGH BOOKS

Grateful acknowledgment is made to the following for granting permission to reprint previously published material: Don Congdon Associates, Inc.: Excerpts from "I Sing the Body Electric" by Ray Bradbury. First published in McCall's. Copyright © 1969 by Ray Bradbury. Reprinted by permission of Don Congdon Associates, Inc.

Mari Evans: "If There Be Sorrow" from *I Am a Black Woman*, by Mari Evans. Published by William Morrow & Company, 1970. Reprinted by permission of the author.

McDougal Littell/Houghton Mifflin Company: Excerpts on pages 96, 97, and 98 from *Responding to Literature, Blue Level*. Copyright © 1992 by McDougal Littell/Houghton Mifflin Company. Reprinted by permission of McDougal Littell/Houghton Mifflin Company, Evanston, IL.

This is a work of fiction. All the characters and events portrayed in this novel are either fictitious or are used fictitiously.

No part of this publication may be reproduced in whole or in part, or in a retrieval system or transmitted in any form or by any means, mechanical, photocopying, recording, or otherwise, without written permission of the publisher. For information regarding permission contact Endicott and Hugh Books. www.endicottandhughbooks.com

ISBN 978-0-9823167-9-5

Copyright ©1995–2011 by Jean Davies Okimoto. All rights reserved.

Cover images
CHEERING CROWD AT CONCERT by Mike_kiev
ASIAN STUDENT by Ver2exe

Published by Endicott and Hugh Books, Burton, Washington

Book design by Masha Shubins

1 3 5 7 9 10 8 6 4 2

Winner of the Parent's Choice Award

"A celebration of diversity."

—*Signal*

"A story of ethnic pride, first love and determination to overcome stereotypes. Okimoto's talents give this book the same wide appeal as her earlier titles *Jason's Women* and *Molly By Any Other Name*."

—*School Library Journal*

". . . humor and empathy that will engage the reader."

—*The ALAN Review*

For Steve and Dylan

TALENT NIGHT

CHAPTER ONE

Last semester, Ivy Ramos sat as far away from me as you can get. If our language arts class were the United States, it was like I sat in Seattle, Washington (where we actually live), and Ivy sat in Key West, Florida. On the first day of class last semester, our teacher, Ms. Leticia Williams, said we could sit wherever we wanted and since it is my tendency to want to dissolve into the wall during class discussions, I chose a seat in the back row. Ivy, on the other hand, was probably born discussing things, she's so good at it. And, in the style of the "in your face with the answers" smart kids, she planted her beautiful body right up front in the first row so she could get called on as much as possible.

The only thing about sitting so far away from Ivy was that I could stare at her through the whole class and she wouldn't see me gawking at her. But basically it meant that if I was ever going to talk to her, it would require my walking across the entire classroom to do it. This was about as realistic as me skipping across the entire continental United States. The result was that all semester, Ivy remained clueless to the fact that I was alive on this planet.

Ms. Williams, besides being a friendly young teacher, was also pregnant. She left a few weeks before the end of the semester to have the baby, which turned out to be a baby girl. She and her husband named it Maya after Maya Angelou and the class sent a pink card that we all signed. We passed the card around all the rows and when my turn came, everyone had signed it but me. I pored over the card looking for Ivy's name. Then I found it, draping around the right corner of the card in beautiful flowy writing:

Congratulations, Ms. Williams, May your daughter always know why the caged bird sings. . . and may poetry live in her heart like her namesake. Ivy Ramos

I remembered a discussion we had in class when we were reading that book by Maya Angelou and Ivy had a lot to say about how important it was for people to understand and appreciate the struggles that their parents and grandparents and everybody who came before them had been through. Ms. Williams tried to stay neutral in these discussions, but you could tell that she completely agreed with Ivy. Not only that, you knew that Ms. Williams liked Ivy best of almost anyone in the class. No one minded, though, because even though you could say Ivy dominated a lot of the discussions, she never acted like she was better than other people. And she never put anybody down when they said dumb stuff.

There was a little room left underneath where Ivy had signed, and I was glad because if I squished my writing, I could fit in there, which was probably as close to Ivy as I would ever get in my life. But I wasn't sure what to write. I was trying to think of something good when the bell rang. So I just scribbled under Ivy's:

Way to go, Ms. Williams! Hope your baby has a nice life.
Rodney Suyama

Then, this semester — which is second semester —I got lucky. We had substitute teachers the last few weeks after Ms. Williams left, but the day second semester started we got our new permanent teacher. His name was Mr. Alexander and he was very different from Ms. Williams. He was a rule guy. He made everyone sit alphabetically. This is where I got lucky. R ... Ramos, next to S. . . Suyama, and I find myself next to Ivy the Beautiful. I thought I had died and gone to heaven.

Our relationship began about pens. Ivy never had one.

"Uh, you got a pen I could borrow?" She looked over at me after digging through her purse and the plastic case clipped to her notebook.

"Yeah — sure." My hand shakes a little as I open my notebook and pull out a red pen. Do I slip it into her hand with a casual half smile (half sexy, half cool — guaranteed to ignite her)? No. I drop the pen, lean over in the chair to pick it up, and the chair tips over.

"Yikes!" I tip back the other way, get out of my seat, and crawl on the floor, groping for the pen, which has now rolled under my chair. I grab the sucker and hand it to her.

"Thanks — uh, what's your name again?"

As I'm getting up from the floor, I hit my head on the desk. Some jerk stuck gum under it, which gets stuck in my hair. As I scramble back in my seat, I try to pull the gum out of my hair.

"Yuk." It's a big wad, all stuck in the middle of my head.

"Yeah, well—thanks, Yuk."

"Huh?" I look over at her, still pulling at my hair.

"Thanks, Yuk."

Then I get it. We have a lot of Chinese kids at our school, and a lot of them haven't been here too long. They're from Hong Kong and Taiwan. Some of the guys have names like Yip and Bok. I know one guy whose name is Bong. She thinks my name is Yuk.

"Rodney."

She gives me a weird look. "My name's Ivy."

"I know. I'm Rodney."

"I thought you said your name was Yuk."

"It's Rodney."

"Oh." She looks confused but just says, "Yeah, well—thanks, uh — Rodney."

I sat there feeling pathetic while she took notes, listening to Mr. Alexander discussing last night's assignment from our Responding to Literature book, a story by a German guy, Heinrich Boll, who won the Nobel Prize in literature. "Action Will Be Taken" was the title and I was sitting there thinking about what action it would take to get the gum out of my hair, imagining that I'd have to cut a big chunk of hair right from the middle of my head, when suddenly I stopped thinking about my hair.

I stared down at my blank paper in silent pleasure, stunned with the realization that Ivy asked me my name. Even though at first she thought it was Yuk, she still asked me. She even said my name, too. At the end of class, she also pocketed the pen.

Later that week, Ivy talked to me again.

"Oh, Rodney, do you have a pen I could borrow?" She smiled sweetly. Ivy's skin is smooth and brown and her dark eyes are huge, like peanut butter cups. Something about Ivy makes me think about food. Ivy's dad is Filipino and her mom is black. I know this because I saw her with them at Parents' Night last semester. So to be technical, she's Filipino American and African American. All I know is with Ivy this adds up to gorgeous.

I whipped out a pen. Then she got embarrassed.

"Oh, I forgot to give you the other one back."

"Don't worry about it."

"Well, okay, thanks." She smiled and took the pen. At the end of class she started to put it in her purse.

Then she laughed, "Ooops, sorry!" She grinned at me and handed it back. "Thanks, Rodney."

Later that day, in study hall, I read the story Alexander had assigned for the next day. It made me feel connected to Ivy, knowing that she had to read the same words.

Studying is not something I usually do in study hall. I write rap — fantastic rap. My ambition is to be the first big-time Asian rapper, a serious rap artist in the great tradition of L.L. Cool J. Totally nineties — relevant, hopeful, upbeat, maybe a few lines about the earth — stuff like that. My cousin Roland Hirada is a musician, at least he was in a band at Roosevelt, but it was basic rock, not rap. I think music runs in our family. Although technically, Roland is my second cousin — his mom is my mom's cousin. Also technically, I'm not all Asian. My dad's white. Ivy and I have this in common. Not the white part, but the fact that we're both biracial. They say birds of a feather flock together. With us, birds of different feathers got together and got us.

But Ivy's parents are still together. Not mine. Incidentally, my exact heritage is half Japanese American and half Polish American, but like a lot of biracial kids who are half white, I think of myself as the half that's not white. Besides, most people assume my sister Suzanne and I are totally Asian (we think our mom's genes blew our dad's out of the water). You could also say Dad himself got blown out of the water, as we've only seen him once since he moved to the East Coast. After he and Mom split up we also dropped him from our hyphenated name. Mom led the charge. No longer was she Helen Suyama-Delenko. Whack! Off went the Delenko ...back to good old Helen Suyama. Suzanne was next. Chop! Down with Delenko. . . suddenly there was just plain Suzanne Suyama. Although plain is not a word you'd use to describe Suzanne. My sister looks like someone in a Nordstrom catalogue, which is where she basically lives—not in the catalogue but in the store (except when she's at work or in class at the U). I was the last to dump Delenko. Maybe it's harder for a guy to erase his dad.

The assignment Alexander gave us was to write a short essay on "After the Ball," a story by Leo Tolstoy. There's not a lot of plot to the story — a man named Ivan goes to a dance, he falls in love with a beautiful lady, he sees the lady with her father, who's an Army colonel, and thinks the father is an okay guy. Then Ivan gets up in the middle of the night to hang around the lady's house and sees that the lady's father is a total slime bucket who's marching around in the dark with Army guys, making them beat the crap out of a poor guy who wanted to split from the Army. After that Ivan doesn't love the lady so much.

The theme of the essay we were supposed to write was, "Does this story confirm or contradict your views about good and evil in people?" So I reread the story to get some ideas. These parts I read several times:

> *It was as though a huge stream had been poured into a bottle which was only one drop short of full — that was how my love for Varenka released all the hidden capacities for love in my heart. I embraced the whole world with my love then. . . and although it seemed to me I was already infinitely happy, my happiness kept growing and growing. We never spoke of love. I never even asked either her or myself whether she loved me. It was sufficient for me that I loved her. The only thing I feared was that something might spoil my happiness.*

I read that and thought about Ivy. I imagined dancing with her, the way Ivan danced with Varenka. (It wasn't that different except probably Ivy and I'd do a little hip-hop first.) *"I would waltz with her for a long time, and she, often out of breath, would smile and say 'Encore,' to me."*

"Again," Ivy whispered, smiling at me and burying her head in my shoulder as I pulled her closer to me, feeling the warmth of her body pressing against mine as we moved together to the hot soul beat. . . YES!

The bell rang. Mr. Ratner, the study hall teacher, opened the door. In the hall, I saw Ivy. Ivy and a guy. Not just any guy. . . she was with Lavell Tyler. Her boyfriend.

Lavell Tyler is the greatest running back ever to play for Franklin. It was only January of our senior year and he already had a full scholarship to the U and would probably be the most famous running back ever to play for the Huskies. People are even talking about him taking his place among the all- time greats. In middle school they said he'd be the next Thurman Thomas …or the next Barry Sanders. His sophomore year he didn't even play jay-vee. He was a starter right off the bat and by the second game of the season against Ingraham, people said he'd be the next Tony Dorsett or the next Earl Campbell. Last year, his junior year, and now this year. . . they say he'll be a Gale Sayers …a Jim Brown. . . an Emmitt Smith …or Sweetness himself, Walter Payton.

Guys like Lavell Tyler don't breathe the same air as guys like me. But my mind is a very powerful thing, because it has the amazing capacity to totally block Lavell Tyler. To actually just block him out. All the times I would think about Ivy Ramos, in my mind there was no Lavell Tyler. The dude didn't exist. It was just Ivy and me.

I stood in the hall and slumped against the lockers, watching Ivy and Lavell out of the corner of my eye. He had his huge arm around her and she was laughing; her head was thrown back, her beautiful teeth gleamed, and her thick, dark hair cascaded down her shoulders.

Standing there in the first floor hallway of Franklin High, my powerful mind failed me, and I found it impossible to block out Lavell Tyler. The undeniable reality of the situation spoiled my happiness. Totally.

But on the way home I stopped at 7-Eleven and bought a bunch of pens anyway.

CHAPTER TWO

Saturday was Fat Tuesday, which is a street fair-type of thing in Seattle that supposedly has something to do with the Mardi Gras in New Orleans. It's fun — there's food, music, artists everywhere. I think the idea of the event is to cheer people up because it can get so gloomy here in February. I went with my two best friends, James Robinson and David Woo, wishing instead I was there with Ivy.

I had to work Saturday morning, but as soon as I got off I went over to David's so I could catch a ride with him and James. Even at work I was thinking about Ivy. I work at the Mt. Baker Cleaners and my sweet thoughts of Ivy that morning took me far away from the piles of rumpled clothes and the stink of cleaning fluid.

Ivy and I had become friends. You'd probably say it was a little one-sided (Ivy talked and I listened) and somewhat limited (it took place only in language arts), but it was a lot better than first semester when she didn't know I was alive. A lot better.

What she talked about basically was Lavell. *Lavell and I went to this party. . . Lavell called me so late last night my mother blew up— totally exploded. . . .Lavell wants to win state this year in the hundred* (last year he ran it in 9.8 when he wasonly a junior). *Lavell didn't call me last night and I was a mess worrying but this morning he said he was at his cousins'. . . .* This last statement was the kind of thing that would give me a flicker of hope. Maybe the guy would just disappear from her life, and Ivy would be free. Free to be mine, all mine. But no such luck, and as the weeks went by, I was so crazy about Ivy that instead of wishing she'd talk about something else (me, for instance), I actually began to enjoy listening to her talk about him. All I did was pretend that I was the great Lavell.

Lavell and I went to this party. (There we were in the dark corner of the basement; the parents were out of town, the music was loud, the beat incessant and driving. . .ta-da boom. . .ta-da boom. . .ta-da boom. . .I sipped my drink. . .ta- da boom. . . ta-da boom. . .Ivy sipped hers. . .ta- da boom. . .ta-da boom . . . then I set my cup down. I took her drink from her and placed it on the table — slowly, deliberately. Then I looked down. Down into the dark depths of her peanut butter cup eyes. I took her in my arms. When we kissed we were eager. . .hungry. . . demanding. And we were there, lost in each other. . .completely unaware of all the other people at the party.). . . *Lavell called me so late last night my mother blew up — totally exploded.* (I lay back on my bed and whispered into the phone, telling her how beautiful she was, how much I wanted her. . .she whispered to me. . .her voice low and sweet, but in the background I heard her mother shriek, shattering the magic between us.). . . *Lavell wants to win state this year in the hundred.* (This year I've got a shot ...I can feel it ...taste it. . .pouring toward the finish line. . .arms held high as the ribbon snaps against my muscular chest. . .state. . .the fastest guy in the whole jammin' state.). . .

Lavell didn't call me last night and I was a mess worrying but this morning he said he was at his cousins'. (I looked down at her and saw the pain in her face, aware of the terrible worry I had caused her by not calling, feeling like a jerk—for a second—for having hurt her, but then she smiled when I told her where I was, and I knew that it would be all right.)

I was hoping that Ivy might be at Fat Tuesday. I kept scanning the crowd but so far I hadn't seen her. James and David and I stopped and got a hot dog. Actually James and I got one each, David got two. David is a very tall guy—I think his grandparents came from northern China where they have some very tall people. David loves to eat, but you'd never know it because not only is he tall, he's also quite skinny. David's been thin his whole life, I think, at least he has been ever since I met him when he and James and I all met in the sixth grade at middle school. We've been hanging around each other ever since.

James wants to be a film director — his heroes are Akira Kurosawa, John Singleton, Matty Rich, and Spike Lee. He worships those guys. He even went out and got glasses like Spike Lee's — not real glasses, because James has good eyes. His pair's made out of window glass. His favorite of all their movies is *The Seven Samurai*. James has seen it thirty-eight times. Every time we go to the video store and we're looking around trying to pick a movie, James grabs *The Seven Samurai*. "How 'bout this one?" he says, like he's never seen it before.

There we were, down in Pioneer Square, strolling by the booths, chomping hot dogs, making jokes. David wore shades even though it was gray out. Then I heard it: The Voice.

The Voice belongs to my mother. Mom and her friend Elaine Shanahan had a booth set up for Fat Tuesday. Mom was wearing jeans and my thick gray turtleneck, which she always borrows for these street-fair deals. Elaine, who is a potter, has wild red hair and wears only black clothes, but is a nice person even if she is a little weird. She and Mom teach art at Infinity, which is a special arts school that's connected to the community college. Although it's not actually at the community college —it's about ten blocks away in a former auto parts store.

Working at Infinity is what Mom considers her day job, a necessity to pay the rent. Mostly, she wants to do her art. It doesn't seem to faze her that there isn't a big demand for aluminum slug sculpture. Her sculptures are enormous, too, a hundred times bigger than real slugs (slimy snails with no shells that crawl around the bushes in the Northwest).

The Voice had gotten louder. My mother had trapped a customer. She leaned out of her booth holding a giant aluminum slug. Except if you didn't know it was supposed to be a slug you would say it was a bunch of aluminum cans hooked together that landed in a Cuisinart and got run over by a semi.

"The Pepsi generation signified all that is young and beautiful, carefree . . . Pepsodent smiles and prosperous America; this Pepsi can has been transformed into a slimy, spineless, lowly creature, which greedily destroys gardens. A metaphor for the destruction of the garden of earth. 'Slug' can also mean a bullet, signifying the violence that is destroying our culture." The Voice was intense, high pitched, Mom was on a roll.

David noticed first. "Isn't that your mother, Su- yama?"

"Yeah." I choke.

"That stuffs art, man?" asks James.

"Yeah, she thinks she's Yoko Ono. . . ha-ha." I laughed, faking a little merriment, praying to be beamed up to another planet.

"This would make a great scene," James said, doing his best imitation of Spike Lee.

"What would?" David popped the last of his second hot dog in his mouth.

"Right here. See, there's this guy who's being chased by the CIA. They think he's a member of Star, the new Mafia in Sicily that's trying to sell uranium to terrorists. But really he sells shoes at Sears and he just looks like the guy they want."

"Let's get a spring roll." David looked over at the Thuy Tien restaurant's stand.

"Then he jumps in your mother's booth and lands in the middle of all those aluminum things. He hides there, then she sees him and does this great karate flip, and whoooom! He flies through the air and lands in the middle of the Cajun band." James gestured toward the band near my mom's booth.

"I think my mother'd mess up your movie."

"Or we could get some of that Thai stuff." David looked across the street. "That chicken with the peanut sauce."

"Right in the middle of those shiny cans—what a great shot!"

"She doesn't do karate."

"There's some New Mexico blue corn tortillas over there." David pointed to the street corner.

We went for the spring rolls. James looked back at my mother's booth. His dark hands framed his face as if he was setting a camera angle, and he squinted through his fake-glass Spike Lee glasses. Besides being into movies, James is serious about martial arts. He has a brown belt in karate. The kind of movies he wants to make are part like Spike Lee's and part like Bruce Lee's. There's always some karate scene in them. . . .But my mother?. . . Now that's weird.

James's mother wears a suit and high heel shoes and works in a bank (she's the kind of mother who would never borrow her son's sweater), and I know he thinks my mother being an artist is pretty interesting. I probably would, too, if I weren't used to it. She's a little bit like a sixties person. With my being into music, wanting to rap and all, I'm probably more like her than Suzanne is.

"It's true, what they say," Mom would mutter when Suzanne went out with another GQ guy in a Beamer. "Hippies beget yuppies. Of course, I wasn't exactly a hippie and let's hope your sister is only temporarily stuck in the eighties." Then she would give me. . . The Look. No words, but that look is a command. *Don't You Dare Go Eighties on Me, Rodney.*

When I got home from Fat Tuesday, I was totally inspired by all the bands and groups that were there. Carib rock, reggae, earth rock, party rock, jazz and blues, alternative rock, southern rock, country rock, doo-wop, Latin salsa, roadhouse blues, hard surf rock, acoustic poets, world groove, trippy, noisy, psychedelic grunge-jazz-metal, smooth jazz, and oldies folk, too. Fantastic!

There were the Hungry Young Poets, Steamy Windows, the Contenders, Shreds, Magic Bus, Hall Aflame, Mother Earth, Jambay, Spike, Mulch, Dog Superior, Radical Arm Saw, Boma Cho, Control Freak, and Strange Fruit. Peace Frog, Meat Hook and Smokie Lonesome, Foundation, Pele Juju, Young Fresh Fellows. . . awesome! It made me really psyched about my music career, and the second I got home I charged down to the basement to practice.

First I checked myself out in the mirror. I have one earring — yep, it's cool. My hair's in a pony-tail. . .definitely cool. I hold an imaginary mike, flip my head back. . .YES!

In the basement, I turn on my drum machine. The rapid-fire pulsating beat shatters the silence and I start jumping around. I'm loose, really loose! I bend over, my back is to the stairs, I wiggle my butt, then leap around — a complete 180!

Suzanne was standing at the bottom of the stairs.

"RODNEY!" she yelled, totally pissed.

Only I couldn't hear her yelling because the drum machine was so loud, but I knew she was screaming at the top of her lungs because her face was red and her mouth was wide open. I went to the machine and turned down the volume. She stomped over and got in my face, glaring at me.

"What is it about the notion of not playing that thing except when there's no one home that's so impossible for you to perceive?

"There's some black goo on your nose."

"What?" She snarled.

"Right there on the end of your nose — some black goo."

Suzanne felt her nose, then looked at her finger. It had a black smudge on it. "I was attempting to put on mascara when that horrible noise made me jump."

"Only trying to be helpful. You wouldn't want to go out looking like that."

"Just give it up, Rodney."

"Huh?"

"An Asian guy can't be a rapper."

"And just why not?"

"You gotta be black," Suzanne sneered with authority. "They're the only guys that are cool rappers."

"Yeah, what about Vanilla Ice."

"He's history. Even you said he was a cheap imitation."

"I could call myself Lemon Ice."

"Like dog pee in the snow," she scoffed, then stomped back up the basement stairs.

Support is a concept not known to my sister, at least not when it comes to me. But at least Mom doesn't discourage me. I wouldn't describe her as enthusiastic; she kind of ignores the whole thing. But being an artist herself, at least she doesn't try to destroy my creativity.

Mom called down the stairs as I was turning off my drum machine."Rodney, I brought a bunch of food home from Fat Tuesday. Come on up if you want some."

In the kitchen, Suzanne was opening the cardboard deli boxes, while Mom carried her sculpture in from the car.

"Want some help?" I asked her.

"No, this is the last one — thanks." Mom carried it through the kitchen to the porch that she uses for a studio. Then she brought in the mail and the paper.

"Yum, dolmades!" Suzanne dumped them out of the box and put them on a plate and stuck it in the microwave.

"How many are there?" I peered in the microwave.

"Two."

Mom leafed through the mail. "You can each have one. I ate on and off all afternoon. There's some coconut cream pie from the Dahlia Lounge in the refrigerator, if you want."

"Did you buy a whole pie?" My mouth began to water as I went to the refrigerator.

"No, it was left over at the end of the day. Tom and Jackie gave it to me."

Tom and Jackie are Mom's friends who own this great restaurant. I love that pie. I would die for that pie.

"Bills," Mom muttered, shuffling the mail, "catalogues, people just trying to get you to buy, buy, buy — no one wants you to conserve." I thought she was about to gear up for her anti-consumption speech when she suddenly got very quiet. I looked over at her and she was staring at one of the envelopes. She held it way out in front of her because she can't read too well without her glasses. They're magnifying-type glasses that she gets in the drugstore. She has half a dozen pairs all over the house but she loses them anyway. Suzanne told Mom she should get a cord like people do with sunglasses and wear them around her neck, but Mom said it wasn't the same as with sunglasses, and she's not ready to look that much like an old lady.

She turned the envelope over and over, holding it way out at arm's length — first looking at the front, then looking at the back, then looking at the front again. All of a sudden, she jumped up and left the kitchen.

The microwave beeped and Suzanne opened its door. "Where's she going?"

"Beats me."

"What was in the mail?" She slid the plate of dolmades out of the microwave. "I suppose you want one of these?"

"You got that right." I took the pie out of the refrigerator. "Want some of this?" Sharing is not my favorite thing with Suzanne, if I have to be honest about it.

"Yeah, I'll cut it—just a little piece."

Good. She's dieting again.

I gave it to her and sat at the table and dug into the pie. I ate the pie first, before the dolmades, following the wise motto of the Pacific Dessert Company: Life Is Uncertain Eat Dessert First.

Mom came back in the kitchen wearing her glasses and reading the letter. She leaned back against the sink, totally absorbed, while Suzanne and I scarfed down the food.

"You sure you don't want some of this?" Suzanne asked her.

No answer. She just kept reading the letter. She seemed to be reading it over several times. Suzanne and I looked at each other, shrugged, and kept eating.

Finally, Mom put the letter down and took off her glasses. "When you're finished, I need to talk to both of you."

We finished eating, rinsed our plates, and sat back down at the table. I tipped my chair back on two legs.

"Don't do that, it makes me nervous," Suzanne snapped.

"I have great coordination. Name one time I fell over."

"There's a first time for everything."

Mom sighed. "Pul-lease, you two." She put her glasses back on, holding the letter in front of her; then slowly, she sat at the table between us. "This is from Uncle Hideki."

"Uncle who?" I asked.

"Uncle Hideki?" Suzanne thought for a moment. "That sounds sort of familiar—I kind of remember that name — I think."

"He's Jiichan's brother from L.A." Mom ran her hand through her hair, which is short with gray in it. When she runs her hand through it, it makes it stick up funny. "He and Jiichan had a fight some years ago and stopped speaking. This is from him—he's eighty now."

"Does he know Baach and Jiichan died?" I asked. My gramma died when I was in the third grade. Baach is a nickname for grandmother in Japanese, the whole word is *obaachan*, and Jiichan means grandfather. He died a year after she did, when I was in fourth grade.

Mom nodded.

Suzanne looked at Mom. "What was the fight about? It must have really been something to make them stop speaking."

"After we left camp our family moved up here, but Uncle Hideki stayed in California."

Mom doesn't talk a lot about when her family was forced to go to the internment camp during World War II. She was a baby then, and they were sent to a camp in Poston, Arizona, for three years. She acts like she doesn't remember much.

"When our family came up here, my father had our names officially changed from Suzuyama to Suyama. He was the oldest, Hideki was his younger brother. They lost everything when they were put in camp, except for a few personal possessions. The one thing of value they had was a sword."

"A sword, like pirates have?" I couldn't imagine Grampa swishing around a pirate sword.

"It was an authentic samurai sword that had been in the Suzuyama family for generations. It was given to Grampa because he was the oldest, and Uncle Hideki was furious because he didn't think my father deserved to have it."

"How come?" This information was amazing to me. Not only was I just now finding out that Suyama was not our rightful name, but back in Japan we had some real samurai ancestors! Incredible. I couldn't wait to tell James.

"Dad changed our name because he thought it would be easier for *hakujin* — white folks — to say it. Uncle Hideki said by changing our name Dad was selling out and therefore he had no right to keep the sword. My father said he was meant to have it even if he'd changed our name to McGillacuddy and he refused to part with it. So Uncle Hideki never spoke to any of us again."

"Where's the sword?" I wanted to know.

"It's in safe keeping at the Wing Luke museum."

"Why's he writing you now, Mom?" Suzanne asked.

"Yeah?" I echoed. "Why now?"

"Here." She handed Suzanne the letter. Suzanne put it on the table between us, I scooted my chair toward her, and we bent over the letter.

Dear Helen,

I have accepted an invitation of the Executive Committee of the Seattle Cherry Blossom Festival to be a judge for their Annual Shodo Exhibition. This year the contest will be held in conjunction with Asian Pacific Heritage month and I am to be in Seattle the weekend of April 19th. I will be staying at the home of one of the committee members, however, I would like to arrange to see you and your children during my stay.

Your Aunt May died this past year and I have inherited $20,000, which was paid to her by the government as reparation for her internment during World War II. I also received the same sum as reparation for my internment. I am revising my will due to this increase in my estate. Since you and your children are my only living relatives, I am considering leaving these funds to the youngest generation of the Suzuyama family, your children.

I stopped at that part and looked at Mom. "He still calls

us Suzuyama — but we're gonna get some green! Man! This is great!"

"What's *Shodo*?" Suzanne asked.

"Calligraphy," Mom explained. "Keep reading."

However, I do not want to leave this money to them if they have not retained anything of their Japanese heritage. I will forever be angry about the pressure many Japanese Americans felt after their internment to deny their heritage. There is an old Japanese proverb, "The nail that sticks up gets hammered down, " but in trying so hard to be American many people went too far! As an alternative to your children, I am considering a bequest to Konishiki, the American yokozuna — or possibly the Nippon Shiitake Society in Nagano, Japan.

I looked up at Mom again. "Konishiki? That 500-pound dude from Hawaii that's the famous sumo wrestler?"

Mom nodded.

"I don't understand." Suzanne looked confused. "If he's so big on everything being Japanese, how come he wants to give his money to a guy from Hawaii?"

"Believe me, I don't pretend to know how Uncle Hideki thinks. The only theory I have is that he's trying to reward an American who has valued something in the Japanese culture."

"Let me see if I get this right—" I jumped up and started pacing around the kitchen. This news was incredible. I couldn't believe what I was hearing. "You mean, this uncle. . ."

"He's your great-uncle."

"He sure is great, wanting to give us money!"

"What's the other thing?" Suzanne asked.

"What other thing?" Mom seemed upset.

"The other thing he might give the money to?"

"We'll get the money!" I slapped my fist against the palm of my hand.

"Shut up, Rodney," Suzanne snarled. "Uncle Hideki didn't say we'd get it for sure. He might give it to that other stuff. He's just considering us. Isn't that right, Mom?"

"That's what it sounds like to me."

"So what is the other thing?"

"It's a Japanese organization of people dedicated to the growth and preservation of shiitake mushrooms." Mom just shook her head, like she couldn't believe this, either.

"We're his own flesh and blood." Suzanne was indignant. "We didn't have anything to do with that sword fight."

"It wasn't a sword fight," Mom growled. "It was a fight about a sword."

"Whatever. . .Rodney and I weren't even born. This is totally unfair."

"Excuse me," Mom growled again. "Exactly where did you ever get the idea that life was fair?"

"Here this long lost uncle shows up with no other living relatives and a pile of money. . . and he's trying to decide between us, some 'shroom freaks, and a fat guy?" I couldn't believe it. This was seriously weird.

CHAPTER THREE

Mom wrote Uncle Hideki back and invited him to come for dinner when he was in Seattle. It seemed like it was a big deal for her to write this letter. She kept starting the letter, then she'd read what she wrote, then she'd tear it up and start over again. This went on for one entire Saturday morning and for a person who is always making little speeches about the environment and conserving resources, she sure used up one big mess of paper.

I was thinking about this guy a lot. Almost anything could get me to think about him. In language arts we were reading a story called, "A Very Old Man with Enormous Wings," by Gabriel Garcia Marquez. This made me think about a very old man with enormous money: Uncle Hideki. Twenty thousand big green ones. . . YES! I could launch my music career, produce a dazzling CD. . . RAP WITH RODNEY (Actually I'd have to get a better rap name.) It would sell millions! At the Grammy Awards I would accept the award with a humble smile. . . *and I would like to thank my Uncle Hideki who made this all possible.*

The bell rang and Ivy came in at the last second. She was

wearing jeans and a black V necked sweater that showed something underneath that sort of looked like a guy's T-shirt. However, there's nothing about Ivy that looks like a guy — and that's not because she wears big hoopy girl-type earrings, either. Her sweater seemed too big for her — it was loose and rumply, but she always wears her jeans so tight they look like they might be painted on her body. This is just one of the many details that I notice about Ivy.

Out of breath, she scrambled to her seat, smiling and holding a card to her heart. "Lavell gave me this beautiful Valentine," she whispered, patting the card tenderly.

"That's nice," I muttered, looking at the card against her chest as long as I could get away with it. She held it out, gave it a soft little kiss, and then tucked it in her purse.

"We're going to divide up into groups today," Alexander announced. "Pair off with the person next to you. I want you to compare Ray Bradbury's story 'I Sing the Body Electric!' with last night's assignment, The Very Old Man with Enormous Wings.'" Mr. Alexander waited while we moved our chairs around. Scrape. . . screech . . . clatter. . . thud . . . bang. . . everybody made a big deal of this, trying to use up as much time as possible on furniture moving as opposed to work. Ivy scooted her chair to the left and I turned mine to face her. I was actually paired with her. Rodney and *Ivy. . . Me. . . Her. . . Us. . . We . . . WE* were a pair. Incredible. Even if it was only for this class. Finally, I'd get to talk to her about something other than Lavell Tyler.

"The Bradbury story is considered fantasy, while the Garcia Marquez story is magical realism. Discuss the elements of each story, how are they different, what seems the same, and prepare a presentation for the class on how they each illustrate the difference between fantasy and magical realism."

"When's it due?" everybody yelled.

"Friday," Alexander said, sitting at his desk taking attendance.

"How long's it gotta be?"

"Hey, what d'ya mean by 'presentation'?"

"Mr. Alexander — is this like a speech or something?"

"Do we *ALL* have to do it Friday?"

"Illustrate — did you mean pictures?"

"I can't draw!"

"This ain't supposed to be art class!"

"Yeah, are we supposed to draw pictures to present?"

People were all yelling at once — which is also a way of not doing any work. None of the yelling seemed to faze Alexander, who looked out the window and scratched his nose. "Everyone should be prepared to present to the class on Friday. I'll select the teams at random" — he scratched his nose some more——"and the presentations will continue into next week. The presentations shouldn't be longer than ten minutes and they should be oral."

"Like a speech?" a bunch of people yelled.

"Correct." Alexander looked down at his book. A lot of people grumbled, including me and Ivy.

"I don't like to talk in front of people," Ivy muttered.

"Me, either."

"I get so nervous. I'm always afraid I'll mess up."

"Same here."

Ivy sighed. "Nike."

"Huh?"

"Just do it. It's a joke in our family. Whenever one of us

kids whines about not wanting to do something, like dishes or taking out the trash. Mom shouts, 'NIKE!'which means 'shut up and just do it.'"

"Nike." I opened my book.

"Right." Ivy opened her book. "Have you read both of them?"

"Yeah."

Ivy leafed through her book. "I liked the one about the electric grandmother — it sure seems different to me than the other one, though."

"Yeah. Wanna list the differences first?"

"Okay." Ivy cocked her head to the side and thought for a moment. All I could think about was how beautiful she was — I wondered how I'd be able to concentrate on the stories. "Well, let's see. In the electric grandmother story, all the people knew how wonderful the grandmother was."

"Except Agatha."

"Yeah, but they all still believed she was a fantastic machine."

"And in the story with the weird angel, nobody knew for sure what he was. Also, the guy who wrote it was from Colombia and he wrote it in Spanish."

"Okay, I'll put that down. Oh — do you have a pen, Rodney?" she asked sweetly.

"Sure." I whipped out a nice blue pen from my stash and handed it to her.

"Thanks."

"Anytime." I smiled.

Ivy started writing and I got out some paper. I figured I'd better write, too, since I was part of the team, even though I would rather just look at her.

"Some people think I know Spanish. They think I'm Hispanic,"

Ivy said, "since my name's Ramos. Mostly they don't know what I am."

"Me, too," I said, remembering when she thought my name was Yuk.

"My grandmother spoke a little Tagalog — one of the languages they speak in the Philippines, that and Ilokano."

"My grandparents spoke Japanese, but I don't know any."

"You're all Japanese?" Ivy asked.

This was the first question she ever asked me about me. It was wonderful. I smiled. "No. My dad's white."

"My mom's black. She learned a few things in Tagalog so she could talk to my grandmother. Once she told me that any way we wanted to talk at home or with our friends was fine, a perfectly good way to talk, but we had to learn this other language, too."

"What language?"

"Green."

"Green language?"

"Green English. How educated people talk, whatever color they are. . . saying 'isn't' instead of 'ain't'. . . stuff like that."

"Why'd she call it Green?"

"Money. Money's green," Ivy laughed. "She said if you want to have a good job you have to know how to talk Green."

The bell rang. Ivy put her paper back in her notebook. "Guess we didn't get too far."

I took a deep breath, screwing up my courage. "Uh — maybe, we could, uh, work on it after school?"

"Sure. Where do you want to do it?"

On a beach. . . a grassy slope. . . my bed. . . "The library?"

"They yell at you for talking."

"My sister and my mom are at work until about five. We could go to my house." I couldn't believe we were having this conversation.

"Where do you live? I have to be home by six."

"Thirty-fourth near Plum."

"Oh," she smiled, "that's not too far from me. Meet me at my locker after sixth period, okay?"

"Great!"

Ivy grabbed her books and turned and walked toward the door. I grabbed mine and they landed on the floor. The suckers slipped right through my grasp. I bent over to pick them up and realized Ivy was gone. Then I panicked. Scooping up my books, I tore for the door and looked up and down the hall. She was already down by Room 206.

"Ivy!" I ran though the crowd like Lavell Tyler running through the Roosevelt High School line.

"Excuse me ...Whoops—sorry —"

"Watch out!" a shrill voice snarled as I bumped a very short person that I didn't even see coming out of Room 200.

"IVY!" I was almost at the end of the hall.

"What?" She finally heard me and looked back, just as she was about to turn the corner.

"Where's your locker?"

"Third floor. Next to Room 307."

The rest of the day crawled, like a flower blooming so slowly you can't see it change (thinking about Ivy was making me more poetic). Click. . . the wall clock in my trig class moved one second after a century of waiting. . . . Click. . . another second after a millennium. . . .I couldn't concentrate on anything except

Ivy, although I finally did get my mind off her by thinking again about my music career.

Uncle Hideki's money would mean that I would really have to take myself seriously as a musician. It would probably be a good idea for me to get some experience as a performer — before I made my CD — since there would undoubtedly be a big worldwide tour to promote it.

After trig, I went to my locker to get my lunch. There were a lot of posters up in the halls advertising the Valentine Dance this weekend. Of course, Ivy would go with Lavell. But I enjoyed pretending that she would dump him once she got to know me this afternoon and that I would be there with her. I would give her a tiny candy heart, the kind with writing on it. It would say, Will You Be Mine? It was either mint green, or maybe soft yellow. Soft yellow, I think. I would take her hand and tell her to close her eyes. Then I would place the heart in the palm of her hand with the writing face up and tell her to open her eyes. Looking down at it, she would smile that dazzling smile and look up at me with her peanut butter cup eyes. "Oh, Rodney. . ."she'd whisper, then, opening her beautiful full lips, she'd pop it in her mouth, sucking it and savoring its sweetness. Then I would pull her to me. . .

"Going to lunch?" David Woo came up behind me, swinging his brown sack.

"Yeah." I looked over at him wearing his shades. "How can you see anything, man?"

"I can see fine, Suyama."

"I'd think you'd bump into stuff."

There were more posters all over the lunchroom. David chomped on his sandwich.

"Wannagotothedance?"

"Huh?" It's hard to understand a guy when his mouth is full of tuna fish.

David wiped his mouth on his sleeve. "Want to go to the dance?"

"I guess so. Does James want to go?"

"Yeah."

"Okay."

I looked at David wearing his shades, scarfing down his sandwich. It would be the same old thing. David, me, and James — rolling into the dance around eleven, slouching against the walls, trying to look cool like we'd just dropped in 'cause we had nothin' better to do. Above it all. Too cool to dance. You'd think by our senior year one of us would have been able to move away from the wall.

On my way to world history I noticed another poster in front of the activity office. FRANKLIN HIGH TALENT NIGHT. The red letters were enormous, with sparkly stuff sprinkled on them. SIGN UP BY FEBRUARY 18th!

I've always wanted to be in Talent Night. Our high school has it every spring, but you have to sign up months ahead of time. Technically, it's very easy to be in Talent Night. They don't have auditions, all you do is sign up. But wanting to be in it and actually signing up to do your talent in front of the whole school are completely different things. My sophomore year, I froze outside the door of the activity office. I got a little farther my junior year: two steps inside the office before I bolted. February 18 was Monday. This was my last chance. Maybe with Uncle Hideki's money backing my CD and the promise of my great music career on the horizon, maybe this year I'd do it for sure. As I had realized earlier, I would need the experience as a performer before I went on tour. I decided to think about it over the weekend.

Walking to my house with Ivy was pure joy. I didn't mind that she talked about Lavell Tyler and the dance and who they were going with and what she was going to wear and the party they were going to after. I just loved being beside her, listening to the sound of her soft voice.

Then I heard an explosion — a loud bang that sounded either like a gunshot or a car backfiring. BANG! There it was again, followed by some sputtering and wheezing as an old dumpy car pulled up. Dumpy is probably too elegant a word for this pile of junk. It bucked along like the choke had gone out and the rear fender rattled, close to falling off. James's car. I knew it well. He was driving and David rolled down the window and leaned out.

"Where ya goin' Rodney?" David yelled, leaning his entire body out the window. Then his shades fell off. "Oh man _ " He got out of the car and bent over to get his glasses, which had bounced against the curb.

As David bent over to get his shades and James was gawking, his eyes enormous behind his Spike Lee fake glasses, I leaned closer to Ivy, my shoulder brushing her and said in a low-cooly-blues-eat- your-heart-out voice, "My place." Ivy and I just kept walking. Those guys sat in the car — mouths hanging open, gaping. Did I think it was necessary to tell them that we were going to work on a project for l.a.? No, I did not. Their eyes were glued to us, staring at us in total shock. I loved it.

When we got to my house, I fumbled my keys and was

so excited to get in the house with her that I couldn't insert the key in the lock. I just couldn't get the stupid thing in the keyhole. It was very embarrassing, but Ivy just looked at the little evergreen tree in the front yard pretending not to notice. I glanced at her and saw her beautiful mouth turned up at the corners like she was a little amused by the situation. But at least she didn't laugh in my face, or say, "Just put the key in the lock, fool!" like some girls might have. Finally, after floundering around for what seemed to be hours, I got the stupid door open and held it for her as she went in.

"This is nice," she said, looking around the living room.

"It's pretty small."

"There's a lot of nice pictures." Ivy looked at the paintings all over the walls.

I helped her off with her coat. My hands brushed her sweater as I lifted the coat away from her shoulders. The butter-soft leather coat felt cool in my hands — but her shoulders had been warm. She raised her arms and ran her hands up from her neck, through the back of her dark hair, fluffing it out, and I wanted to touch her warm brown neck.

Ivy seemed kind of surprised that I had taken her coat as I hung it in the closet. A guy never knows how to act with girls, but I decided it'd be better to try to act polite, with the door and the coat stuff.

"Where'd you get all the pictures?"

"My mom. From her students and her artist friends—she teaches art. They give 'em to her or else she trades."

We went into the kitchen and put our books on the kitchen table.

"Want a Coke?"

"Yeah, great — thanks."

I opened the refrigerator and took out the Cokes. Then I got glasses and put ice in them. This seemed to surprise her, or maybe she thought it was weird. But I was sure you shouldn't just hand a girl like Ivy the can.

"Oh, that's nice," she said, smiling as I handed her the glass. Ivy took a sip. "What does your mom trade for?"

"Sculptures. She's an artist, too."

She looked around. "How many kids in your family, Rodney?"

"Just me and my sister. There's just the three of us, Mom, Suzanne, and me. My dad left a long time ago."

"That's too bad." She sipped her Coke.

"Huh?"

"About your dad."

"Oh. . . yeah, I guess."

"There's six kids in my family — I've got two brothers and three sisters. I'm in the middle." Ivy opened her book to the Ray Bradbury story. "You know what part I liked best in this story?"

"What part?" I opened the book. "What page is it on again?"

"One hundred sixty-four." She turned the pages, scanning the story. "Here it is — this part. It's on page one eighty-two."

I turned to 182 and began to read it from the top, wondering what part Ivy liked so much.

"Read it to me, Rodney — out loud, will you? I like to hear the words. I can think better that way."

I cleared my throat. "Okay, where do you want me to start?"

"The third paragraph from the top —"

"Where it says, 'This above all. . .'?"

Ivy nodded. It seemed a little strange that she wanted me to read it out loud, but if she thought it was the best way for us to do the project, who was I to object? I began:

"'This above all: the trouble with most families with many children is that someone gets lost. There isn't time, it seems, for everyone. Well, I will give equally to all of you. I will share out my knowledge and attention with everyone. I wish to be a great, warm pie fresh from the oven, with equal shares to be taken by all. No one will starve. Look! someone cries, and I'll look. Listen! someone cries, and I hear. Run with me on the river path! someone says, and I run. And at dusk I am not tired, nor irritable, so I do not scold out of some tired irritability. My eye stays clear, my voice strong, my hand firm, my attention constant.

I looked up at Ivy. Her arms were folded on the table and her chin rested on them. "Want me to keep going?"

"Uh-huh," she said, softly.

"'But,' said Father, his voice fading, half convinced, but putting up a last faint argument, 'you're not there. As for love —'

"'If paying attention is love, I am love.

"'If knowing is love, I am love.

"'If helping you not to fall into error and to be good is love, I am love.

"'And again, to repeat, there are four of you. Each, in a way never possible before in history, will get my complete attention. No matter if you all speak at once, I can channel and hear this one and that and the other, clearly. No one will go hungry. I will, if you please, and accept the strange word, "love" you all.'"

Ivy lifted her head, put her elbows on the table and rested her chin in the palms of her hands. She looked straight at me.

"Isn't that wonderful. Don't you wish there was such a thing as a real electric grandmother?"

"It'd be awesome," I said, quietly.

I looked at Ivy and our eyes met. I knew she loved Lavell Tyler, but I knew something else, too. Ivy and I were getting to be friends.

CHAPTER FOUR

Ivy was still there when Mom came home. Sometimes Mom really comes through, and she did that afternoon. She was friendly to Ivy, but the important thing was that she acted very casual, as if I had girls over all the time and it was no big thing. Way to go. Mom!

Ivy and I worked on the project all week at my house, and Mom stayed casual; in fact, she stayed out of the way — which was great. She didn't hang around or run in and out of the living room with a bunch of little unnecessary fake questions so she could see what we were doing. She wasn't snoopy like a lot of mothers.

But toward the end of the week, Mom began to get weird. Every other word was safe sex. How's the presentation coming, Rodney...remember, have safe sex. . . . Pass the rice...remember, Rodney, safe sex. . . . The phone's for you, Rodney. . .remember, safe sex.

"I know all about safe sex. Mom."

"Oh. . . well that's a relief."

"It's when a dog humps your leg."

"RODNEY!"

"It's quite safe. Mom. See, when the dog humps your leg —"

"This is a SERIOUS matter! And YOU are impossible!" she sputtered, and stomped off. It appeared she didn't find my little dog joke so amusing. But at least it shut her up.

Thursday night, Ivy came over to practice our presentation. We had it divided up so I would talk for three minutes on the things that were the same and Ivy would talk for three minutes on the things in the stories that were different. Then I'd talk for two minutes on how Garcia Marquez's story illustrated magical realism and Ivy would talk for two minutes on how Bradbury's story illustrated fantasy. We had each put our parts of the speech on note cards.

"I hope we get picked to do it tomorrow so we don't have to worry about this all weekend," I said, shuffling the cards on the kitchen table.

"Me, too," Ivy said, studying her note cards. "I really hate standing up in front of people." She put her cards down. "Hand me your watch, Rodney. So I can time your speech — mine's too little to see the exact minutes."

I took off my watch and gave it to her. She held it out in front of her. I wanted her to keep it, to have something of mine. . . or maybe I could give her a ring . . . or something with my initials on it to wear around her neck . . . I started daydreaming about this as I looked at her holding my watch in her slim brown fingers.

"Okay, go."

"Huh?"

"Darn. I'll wait till it moves to the next minute. Then start your part."

I looked at my notes. "You know what's really weird, Ivy?"

"What?"

"I get nervous about the idea of making a speech in front of the class, but I work on music— I write rap —"

"You do?"

"Yeah. And the idea of performing doesn't make me that nervous."

"School stuff is different." Ivy put the watch down and looked up at me.

I braced myself. What if she said something cold like Suzanne does about my musical ambitions? I went on the offensive. "My sister says an Asian guy can't rap — only black guys are any good at it."

"And Grace can't be Peter Pan." Ivy smiled. Then she laughed. "Another family thing. My little sister has a book about this black girl in England who wants to be Peter Pan in her school play and the kids tell her she can't because she's black and she's a girl and Peter Pan is white and he's a boy."

"But she gets the part because she's amazing, right?"

"Yeah, *Amazing Grace*. . . have you read it?"

"No. But little kids' books have happy endings."

"It has beautiful pictures, too." Then Ivy smiled again. "I want to hear your stuff."

"Really?"

"Yeah, let's take a break and then when we practice the presentation, you'll be all loose."

Ivy followed me down to the basement and sat on the last stair while I went over to the synthesizer. Except for a light by the washing machine and dryer, the only other one was a light in the ceiling, which I had put on a dimmer switch so I could make the basement seem like a dark club. I turned the light down as dim as it could get so if Ivy looked at me like I was a pathetic and pitiful person, at least I wouldn't be able to see her face.

"This is a new one I just wrote and I only have the first part done," I said to the dark stair. Then I turned to the wall, my back to her as I waited for the right beat, then I whirled around and started.

"She's it/not a wannabe/she's real/not tryin'-t'-be
She's mine/not lyin' to me/not lyin' to me/not lyin' to me
And I see her there/And I want her now/Warm and cool/
She's nobody's fool/
And I want her now/And. I want her now/And I want
her now. . ."

"That's as much as I have." I stopped strutting and turned off the synthesizer and then I went to the dimmer switch. I was shaky as I turned it, afraid that Ivy would know I wrote it about her and that I'd see her on the stairs smushing her face into her arm, laughing into her sleeve.

"Rodney! I wish there was more — that was great!" Ivy beamed.

Excitement is too mild a word for what I felt at that moment. *I will, if you please, and accept the strange word, 'love' you all.* It was magical. . . it was real. . . it was fantasy. . . it was electric. . . .

"Uh, excuse me — I gotta use the bathroom."

"I'll be in the kitchen." Ivy went up the stairs and I followed her, turning into the bathroom in the hall.

Chill! She likes your rap and you can't say anything except that you gotta take a leak? Pathetic!

In the kitchen I sat across from her at the table. "Did you really like it?"

"I loved it." Ivy looked surprised that I had asked, because she's not the kind of person to say things she doesn't mean.

"Monday's the last day to sign up for Talent Night," I told her. "Think I should do it?"

"Most definitely. I think you're really good." It was incredible to have her encourage me like that. Even if she was Lavell's girlfriend, she made me feel like a million dollars.

We timed our speeches and they went really well; they took just a little under ten minutes. And Friday, we lucked out. We were the third team Mr. Alexander called on, which was perfect. We didn't have to go first or second, but we got to go on Friday, so we didn't have to sweat it all weekend. And best of all, Alexander graded them on the spot and handed each team their grade at the end of class. The famous team of Ramos and Suyama aced it!

But the weekend after the project was over was lousy. I was really bummed, thinking that from then on I'd only get to see Ivy in class. No more walking home from school. No more Ivy in my basement. No more Ivy watching me rap. No more sitting and talking around the kitchen table. I wished that we hadn't been picked to do it on Friday, because now there was nothing to look forward to.

Saturday, after I got off work at the cleaners, I spent the rest of the day in the basement working on my music. Every rap I wrote turned into blues, full of pain and loneliness. . . .

*rain in my heart/my eyes really smart/wishin' it was you/
the wound in my soul/crashin' down an empty black hole/
my body like lead/nothin' but dread. . . .*

It was pretty depressing stuff.

I think Mom and Suzanne figured out the situation, even though I never said anything. Sometimes our family is good at knowing how someone feels without anyone having to spell it out — we kind of sense things about each other. That afternoon, Suzanne didn't yell at me for practicing when she was home. In fact, when I finally emerged from the basement, she asked me if I wanted to go out and get a pizza with her. She can be nice when she wants to. Also, Mom offered to let me have the car — but I didn't need it, since James was coming to pick me up.

James and David came by and we went over to James's house to watch a video. Surprise. He'd picked out *The Seven Samurai.*

"Check this out," James said, stopping the video. "See this scene?"

"We've seen it," David mumbled.

"Twenty-seven times." I slouched back on the couch, folding my hands behind my head.

"See where the samurai are planning their strategy to defend the farmers?"

"Yeah, what about it?" David pulled his shades down on his nose and peered over them.

"The head guy—he's got a baby on his lap."

"So what?" I said.

"Name one American movie, a western or war movie or cop

thing, where the head guy is making fight plans with a baby on his lap."

David and I just sat there—we couldn't think of any.

"See, in American movies, a guy holding a baby would make him a wimp. But in Kurosawa's movie the guy can be tough and still hold a little baby. It's very subtle," James said, in his artsy film director voice, "but it's cul-tur-al."

David looked at his watch. "Want to go to the dance?"

"Don't you want to see the rest?"

"We know how it ends." I got up and stretched. "Let's go over to school and check it out."

James knew when he was outnumbered. "I don't know why I waste my time. You guys have no appreciation of the art of filmmaking." He rewound the movie and we left for the dance.

We rolled in at eleven like we always do, strolled around casually, and then slumped against the gym wall.

I scanned the dance floor until I found Ivy. She and Lavell were dancing so slow and squished together it was hard to tell when Ivy began and Lavell left off. . . .

rain in my heart/ my eyes really smart/wishin' it was you/ the wound in my soul/crashin' down an empty black hole/ my body like lead/nothin' but dread. . .

My crappy rap came back to me; it hurt to watch them.

The song ended and Ivy and Lavell crossed the gym floor, passing by us on their way out to get some fresh air. He had his arm around her. She looked beautiful in her deep burgundy red dress.

"Hi, Rodney." She smiled as they passed us.

"Hi." I tried not to sound as miserable as I felt.

"You and Ivy sure hung around together a lot last week," James said, watching Ivy and Lavell.

"Fantasy and magical realism," I mumbled.

"Huh?" James asked still watching her. "Man, that girl looks good."

"Sure does." David practically drooled.

"Fantasy and what did you say?" James turned back to me.

"We had to compare them — it was a school thing."

"You still working on it with her?"

"It's over."

On Monday I looked at the poster about signing up for Talent Night. I was still bummed from my project with Ivy ending, and it made it even harder to get up the nerve to go to the activity office. I tried to go in before homeroom but never made it. At lunch I walked by a few times but couldn't get myself to go in. Now school was out and I had fifteen minutes to get there before the activity office closed. "This is your last chance, Rodney," I said to myself as I slammed my locker door. I wandered the halls for a while, looking at my watch. Finally I got to the hall where the activity office was.

"Get a grip," I said to myself as I paced back and forth outside the door. "Your career in the entertainment business will be history if you don't even start it." I closed my eyes, picturing Ivy, remembering what she had said when I asked her if I should sign up for Talent Night. Most definitely. . . I could almost hear her soft voice. . . I think you're really good.

Finally, with two minutes left, like the two-minute warning

in a football game, I went into the activity office. Nike. . . as they said in Ivy's family.

Ms. Washington, the activity coordinator, was closing the top drawer of a file cabinet.

"I'm closing up," she said when she saw me.

"Do I still have time to sign up for Talent Night?"

She pulled a file out of the drawer. "Oh, I suppose." She sounded disgusted. "But I don't see why you kids all wait till the last minute. I've had ten kids in here in the last twenty minutes."

She opened the folder and took out a sheet and put it on the desk. I looked at all the names. A lot of them I didn't recognize but there were some I did. . . Katie Klein and Amy Kirkman, June Kubo, Tina Mandapat, Cissy Caver, Joel Ing, Peggy Washburn, Mian Rice, Dana Jones, Michael Johnson, Stephen and Dylan Au, Richard Garcia, Jim Robert, Pham Saephan. . . I would be the last one, on line thirty- seven.

"Remember, no pets," Ms. Washington instructed.

"Huh?"

"We don't allow any animals in your act," she reminded me, "not after last year when Jonathan Westover and Mark Jacobson wanted to do Stupid Pet Tricks and the janitors almost went on strike."

I had forgotten that. The brand new stage was knee high in dog doo.

"And no juggling breakable objects."

"Okay." I reached in my pocket for a pen.

"All acts are limited to three minutes."

No pen. I had given my last one to Ivy. "Uh, Ms. Washington, can I borrow a pen?"

She shoved a pen at me, I looked down at the blank line across from number thirty-seven, and by some miracle I got the nerve. I actually signed my name right there on the line. Rodney Suyama.

"We have to have everything ready to print the program three weeks before Talent Night." Ms. Washington took the sheet and put it back in the file. "So if you want your act to have a name be sure to get it in on time."

"Okay, thanks."

On my way home, I stopped in at the Colonel's to see David Woo. He works there after school. I got a piece of chicken and a biscuit. I wanted to tell him about signing up for Talent Night, but it was pretty crowded and David didn't have time to talk. I sat at a table, munched my chicken and looked out at the cars going by on Rainier. It had started raining and they all had their headlights on. The rain swept over the window, making diagonal lines across the pane. Sitting there watching the lights of the cars go by, I thought about Ivy, wishing she had been with me when I had signed up for Talent Night. I wondered if I'd ever see her again outside of school. It seemed like being with her and then having it end was even worse than how it had been before I knew what it was like to hang around with her. I waited for the rain to stop and when it had slowed to a drizzle, I went outside, waved to David, put my collar up, and headed home.

By the time I got home, Mom and Suzanne had finished eating. They were sitting at the kitchen table drinking coffee.

"There's some spaghetti left, if you want —" Mom motioned to the pot on the stove.

I dumped some spaghetti on a plate and joined them at the table. Mom looked kind of sad.

"Her grant was turned down," Suzanne said quietly.

"That's really too bad," I said as I slurped the spaghetti. Poor Mom. Stuff like that happens to her a lot. She'd applied for a grant from the King County Arts Commission to do a big installation piece of her aluminum slug sculpture. At least with Talent Night they have to let anybody who signs up be in it.

"Art is not a profession where one has to invent new ways to be disappointed." Mom sipped her coffee.

Mom acts brave, but Suzanne and I both know it always gets her down when her stuff gets rejected.

"They're stupid not to give you the grant," I said.

"Rodney's right. What do they know?"

"Thanks." Mom got up and went to the stack of mail on the counter. "This came today." She handed me a letter. "Suzanne already read it."

I opened the letter.

Dear Helen,

Thank you for your dinner invitation. I accept your invitation and will look forward to seeing you and your children.

Yours truly, Uncle Hideki

"When is he supposed to come here again?" Thinking about his visit was definitely cheering me up.

"The Cherry Blossom Festival is the third week in April. He's coming for dinner April twentieth."

"So he's really coming! This is serious!" I had been dreaming about getting the money, but now it seemed much, much more real. Signing up for Talent Night was the first big step. But when I got that money, I'd really be on my way!

"I want to open a karaoke club that has regular fashion shows. My own business — it would be totally unique, nothing exists like it. A surefire success!" Suzanne's cheeks flushed with excitement.

Mom abruptly got up from the table. She turned away from us and furiously began scrubbing the dishes in the sink. Then she snapped on the radio by the sink. It was turned to her favorite oldies station. "*I've seen fire and I've seen rain*," James Taylor wailed, louder than Mom ever has the radio.

"What's wrong with her?" I whispered to Suzanne.

Suzanne shrugged.

"Mom —" I raised my voice, trying to get her to listen to me over James T. "We really do think it's lousy about your grant."

Mom spun around and glared at us. "You kids have been so busy dreaming about the money, I think you forgot what he said in his earlier letter," she snapped.

Suzanne and I stared at each other.

"I guess I just conveniently forgot that this isn't a done deal," Suzanne admitted.

"Me, too. So, uh, we're supposed to show him that there's something Japanese about us. Right?"

Mom nodded.

There was a long silence. Suzanne and I just kept looking at each other. We each went blank at the same time — maybe this wouldn't be so easy. Suzanne tapped the table with her red nails. I leaned back on the legs of my chair.

"Don't do that — you'll tip," Suzanne said absentmindedly.

"It helps me think." Then I sat forward, banging the front legs of the chair down. "I know," I piped up. "I've got a great idea. When he comes for dinner —I'll make Top Ramen!"

CHAPTER FIVE

I vy's seat was empty. The bell rang and Mr. Alexander closed the door. It wasn't like her to be late to class. In fact this whole semester I couldn't think of a single time that she'd ever been late.

It seemed like half the school had the flu this month and I started worrying that she might be sick. Poor Ivy. Lavell would be too busy with sports after school and so I'd be the one to go over to her house to take care of her. I'd bring her some nice clam chowder from Skipper's on Rainier. She'd lie back, the curls of her beautiful dark hair cascading over the smooth white pillow. "Oh, Rodney, thank you for bringing this soup."

I'd stroke her forehead and gently kiss her.

"Oh, you might get germs," she'd say, concerned for me.

"Think nothing of it," I'd say, softly kissing her cheek. "Now get some sleep." And I'd sit next to her bed, cradling her hand in mine, watching her as she lowered her black curly lashes, slowly closing her dark peanut butter cup eyes.

I looked at her chair; still no Ivy. Language arts was the highlight of my day, of my life, to be accurate. Ever since our presentation, I kept hoping Alexander would assign another one— longer, like maybe a twenty-minute thing, or even a half hour, so we'd have to meet at my house for months. But so far he hadn't, which meant that I had to be satisfied with just seeing Ivy in class. Without her, I couldn't care less about that class.

The last few weeks we had been working on Unit Four, Poetry. Last week we read a poem by Anne Sexton called "Oysters." Ivy and I agreed about oysters: we didn't like them. Unless they were fried, like you get down on the waterfront at Ivar's. When we read "If There Be Sorrow" by Mari Evans, it made me quite sad. The poem went like this:

If there be sorrow let it be
for things undone undreamed
unrealized
unattained
to these add one:
love withheld
restrained

Alexander had different people in the class read the poems out loud, then we would discuss them. He picked Stephen Wong to read the one about sorrow. Stephen read it well. He has a nice voice and as he read, I thought some more about Ivy, wondering if she even had a clue how I felt.

"Today we'll discuss Shakespeare's sonnet, 'My mistress' eyes are nothing like the sun/ " Mr. Alexander announced.

This is the kind of poem that if you had to read it in junior high or middle school the whole class would crack up when somebody had to read the line, "If snow be white, why then her breasts are dun." But since this is senior l.a., there was only one smirk by Jonathan Westover, who is a jerk. (He's the same guy who had his dog do a Stupid Pet Trick at Talent Night last year, which ended up stinking up the auditorium.)

While Norman Schwartz was reading the last line,

"And yet, by heaven, I think my love as rare As any she belied by false compare."

Ivy came in the room. She scurried to the back of the class and slumped into her seat next to me, looking like someone had died. Her eyes were nothing like the sun. She was blowing her nose, sniffling; her beautiful dark eyes were practically swollen shut from crying.

"Ivy. . . what's wrong?" I whispered.

"That witch. . . *sniff, sniff,* that witch *sniff,* witch *sniff,*" she mumbled, dabbing her eyes.

Alexander glared at us, so Ivy put her head down on her desk. I just sat there, trying to figure out what had happened, pretending to pay attention to Dana Lovelett, who was reading "Ye tradeful merchants, that with weary toil" by Edmund Spenser. Ivy seemed as mad as she was sad, so I was pretty sure no one had died.

When class was over, Ivy stayed in her seat while everyone got up to leave. "Rodney, stay with me."

Music, that's what those words were. Pure poetry. I cemented my butt to the chair.

When the class had emptied out, Ivy slowly stood up. "Take me to Burger King, will you, Rodney? I can't face that lunchroom."

As we walked out of the building, Ivy started to cry again. I wasn't sure if I should, but I put my arm around her. It just seemed like the right thing to do. Also, the fact that I actually did it might have been because I had imagined holding her so often. Sort of like how they tell athletes to visualize winning, running the perfect race, stuff like that. Sports psychology. Well, maybe all my fantasies of Ivy were like that, so when the opportunity came, I was ready. All I know is whatever made me put my arm around her was good because it was the right move. I knew this because she didn't pull away. She leaned her head into my shoulder, making soft little sniffing sounds.

At Burger King, the whole story came out. Ivy and four other girls from her family psychology class went to John Muir, the elementary school near Franklin, to observe kindergarten kids for something they were learning about child development. On the way back she saw none other than Lavell Tyler in the front seat of Deleisha Johnson's car kissing Deleisha Johnson.

"I felt like a total fool! There he was in broad daylight, kissing that girl. That witch!"

"That's terrible," I said sympathetically.

"Then when I saw him before class and let him have it—he had the nerve to tell me to be understanding and that he just wanted to see us both! I told him what he could do with that idea!"

"So you broke up?" I tried not to sound cheerful.

"Of course! No way am I putting up with that boy's crap! I want a guy who'll be reliable, you hear what I'm saying, Rodney?"

Reliable Rodney, that's what they call me. From then on Ivy and I were inseparable. I walked her to class, carried her stuff, picked her up at her job — sometimes on Saturdays she'd even come to the Mt. Baker Cleaners just to say "Hi." I would be there bundling up and tagging people's smelly, stained clothes and in would walk Ivy, a breath of fresh air. It was wonderful.

Although we never really defined our relationship, we were more than friends, but I don't think she thought of me exactly as her boyfriend. Whatever it was, I was the first guy on the spot after Lavell and it was probably a rebound thing. But so what? Who cares? I got to be with her. And little by little it did get a bit more physical. I'd put my arm around her, we'd give each other back rubs . . . nothing too heavy, but nice. . . very nice.

But one thing about my physical relationship with Ivy was that she got closest to me when Lavell was in sight. As soon as she'd see him coming down the hall, she'd grab my hand and walk along holding it, looking into my eyes and smiling as if we were the only two people in the world.

In fact the one time we did kiss was when we were walking by the track after school. The track team was working out and Lavell was warming up, stretching on the grass, his muscles bulging all over the place. As we got opposite him, Ivy stopped, slipped her lovely brown arms around my neck, lifted her face, and brushed my mouth with her sweet soft lips. Then she slowly pulled away, took my hand, and led me down the side-walk because I was dazed and could hardly walk. Did I mind that this was probably for the benefit of Lavell Tyler? No, I did not. I'm not a proud person and I would take Ivy on any terms, any terms whatsoever.

Ivy helped me, too. It wasn't just all one-sided.

She kept encouraging me about my music career and when the deadline was almost up to have your act named for Talent Night so they could put it in the program, Ivy insisted that I get a good name.

"There's nothing wrong with Rodney Suyama, but you just need a different rap name," Ivy said with a serious look on her face.

"I agree."

"We'll have to really concentrate on this over the weekend."

"For sure."

The next Saturday I met Ivy when I was through at the cleaners and we decided to go to Baskin- Robbins for ice cream. We stood at the counter looking at the names of the flavors, trying to decide what to get.

"Hey, Rodney." Ivy seemed excited. She pulled a little notebook out of her purse and started writing down names of flavors. "We could get you a name from here!"

"Huh?"

"A good rap name." Ivy studied the list. Then she wrote down some names. "I guess there are only two that could work."

I read over the list of flavors, not really sure what Ivy meant. "Which two?"

"Seems like the name should reflect that you're an Asian rapper—so I put down Lemon Surprise and Banana Delight."

We got our ice cream — we both got chocolate chip and walked up Rainier, heading for Mt.

Baker Park. It was a beautiful day, warm for early spring. Little green buds were popping out on the bushes and cherry trees were beginning to bloom. I loved walking along next to Ivy licking that chocolate chip. Ivy stopped and laughed. Some of her ice cream had dripped on her chin.

"What a mess," she laughed as the bottom of her cone got all squishy. She popped it in her mouth. I took my napkin and wiped the ice cream off her chin.

"Thanks, Rodney." She smiled her sweet smile.

At the park we sat on the grass on the slope behind the tennis courts. Ivy took out her notebook and looked where she had written those two flavors.

"What do you think of MC Lemon Surprise?"

I lay back on the grass, folding my arms behind my head imagining an announcer saying, "And now, by popular demand, ladies and gentlemen, we bring you MC Lemon Surprise!" I thought about it awhile. "I don't know, Ivy, it doesn't seem quite right."

Ivy sat next to me chewing a blade of grass, looking down at the notebook in her lap. "How about Almond Joy?"

" A candy bar?" I sat up.

"'Cause your eyes are almond-shaped?"

"It's chocolate on the outside," I reminded her.

"Oh, right. . . hmmm." Ivy hesitated, thinking. "How about Golden Raisin …or Lemon Drop. . . hey—how about Golden Wheat?"

"Isn't that a cereal? How come we gotta name me a food?"

"We don't have to. Hey, how about Havana Banana?"

"I dunno. . . sounds like I'm Latino. Besides, banana had a bad connotation, like you weren't really Asian."

I lay back on the grass and folded my arms behind my head again, looking up at the sky for some inspiration.

"Oh, yeah, Asian on the outside and white on the inside." Ivy picked at the grass. "I'm telling you if I got worried about stuff like that it'd make me crazy. Like I wouldn't be cool enough to be black since I'm half Filipino or vice versa." She sighed. "I can't be bothered with that. Now what do you think, how 'bout DJ Lemon Drop?"

"I like Havana Banana better — but people would probably think I was a wannabe Latino." I thought about this for a minute. "Actually, being Latino would be cooler than half Japanese and half Polish."

"What's wrong with it? That's what you are."

"Nothing. You're just not all one thing, that's all. Doesn't being mixed bother you?"

"I have this cousin on my dad's side. He's in the Aces —"

"That Filipino gang?"

"Yeah. He's a real loser. But my grandmother won't give up on him and sometimes we see him at Christmas. I'm surprised he's not dead yet. Anyway, he has a real thing about being with anybody who's not Filipino — he gives me a bad time. First about Lavell—then the other day he hassled me about hanging around you."

"Me!" I was flattered, but I have to admit — it also kind of blew me away. "Most people think I'm all Asian. What's this guy do, check out birth certificates?"

"You're not Filipino. That's the whole thing with him."

"So you're only half —"

"Did I say this jerk hassling me made sense?"

Then I had an idea. "Hey — why not something with *hapa*?"

"Hapa? People who are half?"

"*Hapa haole*. . .Hawaiian for half white."

"I thought it meant anybody who's half Asian."

"Now it does. It just came from *hapa haole*." I was beginning to like this whole concept. "What do you think? MC Hapa? Or DJ Hapa?"

Ivy smiled. "Hapa Poppa?"

"I don't think so." Then I sat up. "I know, I've got it! Ice Hapa."

"That's not bad, Rodney. Not bad at all."

"Okay, Ice Hapa it is."

After I got home from the park, Suzanne pulled up with her latest boyfriend. She kissed him and then hopped out of his car. This guy drove a Mazda MX-6, a departure from most of the guys she dates, who all seemed to drive BMWs. Sometimes I think Mom's right, Suzanne got stuck in the eighties. I can never keep track of her boyfriends. She seems to trade them in on new models quite often, so I just call them all "the white guy."

Suzanne came in and put her packages on the couch, a couple of Nordstrom bags.

"So, you went shopping with the white guy?"

"His name happens to be Brent Hanson," Suzanne said icily.

"How come you never date Asian guys, anyway?" I asked.

"How come you never date Asian girls?" Suzanne spat back.

"Ivy's half. Anyway, Asian girls are bossy."

"Asian guys are boring."

Mom came into the living room from her studio. "What are you two arguing about?"

"Rodney says he doesn't date Asian girls because they're bossy and I said I didn't date Asian guys because they're boring," Suzanne reported.

Mom shook her head. "Uncle Hideki's not going to be ready for this family — and it's not just you kids."

"You and Nate?" Suzanne asked.

"Uh-huh." Mom smiled.

Nate's Jewish. Mom's been going out with him on and

off for years. Then I had this great idea. "Maybe when Uncle Hideki comes we could invite some people over who are one-hundred percent Japanese American. Or maybe some people from Japan — we could pretend that's who we date!"

"Bring in ringers?" Suzanne asked.

"We could raid the youth group at Seattle Buddhist church."

"That's ridiculous," Suzanne snorted. Then she thought for a minute. "But actually, there's a guy that went to high school with me at work — Dave Fujii."

"How come you've never talked about him?" I asked.

"I don't know him that well."

"Yoshiko Maeda is an exchange student from Japan in my class. I could ask her for dinner." I thought this was a great plan.

"How well do you know her?"

"I've only talked to her a couple of times," I admitted.

"It'd be hard to pull off," Suzanne thought, "trying to pretend we're involved in relationships with people we hardly know."

"You kids can't just ask Brent and Ivy to disappear for a few days," Mom snapped. "It's not right!"

Suzanne and I looked at each other and both nodded. It would be a rather slimy thing to do.

"Maybe we could learn a few words of Japanese," Suzanne piped up. "Let's make a list of all the ones we know." She ran into the kitchen and came back with some paper and a pencil. "Baach and Jiichan," she began.

"I don't think you should write those down because even though it means Gramma and Grampa — they're names. It's not exactly like they're words." We had to do this right, I decided.

"So — then you go first, Rodney."

"*Sayonara.*"

"That's good, okay let's see — " She chewed the end of the pencil.

"*Arigato,*" she said, writing it down.

"That means 'thank you, right?'"

"Yeah, but it's short for something; I can't remember the whole thing."

"*Arigato gozaimas,*" Mom said, sounding annoyed.

"*Arigato gozaimas,*" Suzanne and I repeated together while she wrote it down. "Okay, Rodney. What else?"

"*Sushi.*"

"Good." Suzanne put that down. Then she looked discouraged. "Gosh, I can't think of anything else, can you?"

I sat there and thought. "I guess that's it ... *Sayonara. . . arigato. . . sushi.* Not much of a vocabulary."

"Pitiful."

Then I started to laugh.

"It's not funny, Rodney. I have my heart set on having my store. I think about it all the time — wonderful fashions for Asian Pacific women, all petite sizes, local as well as international designers, me singing with the karaoke machine while the models show the clothes, there'll be a fantastic logo on the shopping bags. . . we've got to do better than *sayonara, arigato,* and *sushi!*"

"*Honda.*"

"Huh?"

I laughed even harder. "*Honda. . . Nissan. . . Toyota. . . .* "

Suzanne started to laugh. "*Mitsubishi. . . Sony. . . .*"

"Remember that old pop song called 'Sukiyaki'?" I laughed some more. We both started to hum it, even though we didn't know any words. "Well, you can make it sound like a Japanese song." I started singing to the tune.

"To. . . yo . . . ta, Nis. . . san, Hon. . . da Mi. . . tsu . . . bi . .
• shi, Ni. . . kon, Maz. . . da Ya. . . ma. . . ha, Hi . . . ta. . .
chi(ee), Son . . . y,
Su. . . zu(oo) . . . ki(ee) Su. . . ba. . . ru, Ra. . . men, Su. . .
shi, Son. . . y I. . . chi. . . ban, I . . . su. . . zu, Sa. . . shi. . . mi"

Suzanne got the idea and sang it with me. We were in hysterics. We started jammin' around the living room singing, and Mom cracked up watching us.

But Suzanne stopped singing when we got to the line where we sang, "Ramen."

"You know, Rodney," she said very seriously,

"when Uncle Hideki comes, I think we'd better try to cook a real Japanese dinner and not just have Top Ramen."

"Good idea — except for one thing. We don't know how."

Suzanne looked at Mom, hoping she might help us out. But Mom suddenly got quiet.

Finally she said, "I don't want any part of this. I won't stand in your way, but you two will just have to decide together how you want to handle his visit." Then she left and went back to her studio. She seemed upset.

CHAPTER SIX

On my way to language arts I noticed a lot of posters up in the halls advertising the upcoming dance. COME TO THE SPRING THANG! APRIL 7th. . . LIVE MUSIC! This was unusual; they usually just have a dj at our school dances. The band would probably be crummy, since the junior class was putting on this dance and they don't have much money. People don't get serious about the class treasury until senior year, when everyone wants a good band for the Senior Prom. The live music at the Spring Thang would probably be somebody's garage band. My cousin, Roland Hirada, had a garage band when he went to Roosevelt a couple of years ago — I think he had a couple of gigs at the school—but he gave up his band when he got to the U. Not enough time, I guess.

I was determined that my rap career wasn't going down the toilet like Roland's rock band. Thinking about this made me remember that I'd have to get to the activity office to sign up my rap name so they could put it in the program. I'd do it during lunch, write it down there in big letters: ICE HAPA. . .YES!

There was another poster advertising the Spring Thang right outside our l.a. class. I stopped and looked at it for a minute before I went in. Maybe I could ask Ivy. Wow. What a thought! Now with Lavell out of the picture, maybe she'd like to go with me, good old reliable Rodney.

Even though Ivy and I were hanging around all the time, I still didn't know if she thought about me as anything really more than a friend. I mean, most of the physical stuff still would only happen in the presence of Lavell—except those nice times with the back rubs when we'd be studying at my house. I can't say they were romantic back rubs, more like a buddy thing. But maybe if I asked her to the dance it would give our relationship the little shove it needed. Thrust it right out of the friendship ball park, get to first base with Ivy or hit a big homer for love! (I had watched one of the Mariners spring training games the night before — they seemed to be as pitiful as ever, except for Junior, but I'm a die-hard M's fan — I guess that's why I was thinking in baseball terms that morning.)

I could just see us at the dance, Ivy dazzling in emerald green, me wearing jeans, a white T-shirt, and a big flowered green tie — definitely cool. Maybe a little green earring instead of the little gold one I've got. The garage band would not be terrible, it would be a great R&B band, perfect for slow dancing in dark corners. Lavell would be there with Deleisha Johnson and I would maneuver Ivy and me next to them. Ivy would look up at me and we'd kiss, hot and heavy, one of those "in your face, Lavell" kisses. But then, something would happen. Lavell and Deleisha would leave, and Ivy would keep kissing me. ZAM! Like lightning, she'd be struck with the realization that it was me, Rodney, that she loved all along. Then we'd go out to the parking lot. We'd drive down to Mt. Baker Beach and park by the lake. I'd move away from the steering wheel, take her in my arms. Maybe we'd get in the backseat. It would be wonderful. . . Ivy and me, melting into each other. . . Ivy and me. . . together. . . forever. . . Ivy and m — Uh-oh. I am not in the backseat with Ivy. I am about to enter Room 257. I am about to be very embarrassed walking into this class if I don't get my mind out of the backseat. . . out of the backseat and on to something else. . .like, like. . . batting averages. Good idea. Ken Griffey, Jr., .314. Jay Buhner, .282. Omar Vizquel, .268. Tino Martinez, .265. Dave Valle, .243. Ken Griffey, Sr. . . was it .300 when he retired or .304? I was trying to remember as the bell rang.

It was weird walking into class. I thought everyone was looking at me, like they all knew what I had been thinking. I sat down next to Ivy and immediately got out my book, leafing through it like I had to seriously look up something. I was still trying to chill out and didn't dare look at her. What I had been imagining was too intense.

"Rodney?" Ivy cocked her head and looked at me. "Aren't you going to say 'hi'?"

"Oh, yeah, hi." I grinned, feeling embarrassed, like she'd read my mind, too.

"What's the big deal in the book?"

"What?"

"You seem psyched — we're not having a test today, are we? Did I miss something?"

"No — I've got to find this poem." I leafed through the poetry section trying to find something I could say about a poem that would make sense to get me out of this. Then, I actually did. I couldn't believe it, but there was this poem in the haiku section by this old Japanese guy. It was just the kind of stuff I'd need to know to impress Uncle Hideki.

"Great! Here it is!" I looked down at page 512.

"There's what?" Ivy looked over at my book.

"It's a haiku poem by Matsuo Basho ——"

Ivy got out her book and turned to the same page. "You mean this one about the frog? Why do you need a frog poem, Rodney?"

I started to tell her, but then Alexander called on Diane Nilson to read "Horses Graze" by Gwendolyn Brooks.

"A perfect choice," Ivy whispered. I nodded in agreement. Diane Nilson was a horse-faced, rich plastic girl that we both couldn't stand.

After class Ivy and I decided to eat lunch outside on the steps by the south lawn. We didn't get our coats, it was so warm — almost sixty-five degrees. Usually it doesn't get over sixty until April.

"So how come you need a frog poem?" Ivy pulled her sandwich out of her lunch sack.

"My uncle Hideki's coming to check us out." I took a bite of my apple. Then I told her the whole story about the reparations money.

"Your mom was in one of those camps, too, wasn't she?"

"Yeah, from when she was a baby until she was three years old."

"Does she get the money?" Ivy asked.

"I think so, but she doesn't really talk about it."

"I think the government should give money to all the people that have been screwed over. Made slaves, put on reservations — you know, everybody."

"Me, too. But I think it has to do with how the legal system

64

works. The Japanese Americans were American citizens who were imprisoned without due process — so it was against existing laws."

"And slavery was legal at the time they made people slaves and they weren't citizens," Ivy said.

"Yeah, I think that's why the Japanese Americans could get this reparations money."

"Well, maybe the government will think twice before they round up people because of what they look like and take all their stuff and throw them in camps." Ivy finished her sandwich and scrunched up her bag. "They never threw the German Americans in camps or the Italian Americans and we were at war with them, too."

I looked over at the gym. Lavell Tyler was walking toward the door of the men's locker room. I knew Ivy noticed him, because she scooted over closer and leaned against me. I'd have to ask her, I'd have to ask her right now, or else maybe I'd never get up the nerve.

"Ivy?"

"Hmmm?" She looked up at me adoringly.

"Want to go to the Spring Thang with me?" There, I'd said it. Didn't choke, I really said it. Ivy kept looking up at me but didn't say anything.

"Ivy?"

"Hmmm." She smiled up at me, then glanced out of the corner of her eye at Lavell. When he disappeared into the locker room, Ivy moved away a little and looked down at the steps.

"Did you hear what I said?" I asked.

"I just don't think I'm ready for it, Rodney. I really like being with you and our friendship is important to me — but it's just too soon for me to have to see him with Deleisha." Ivy looked apologetic. "I'd rather not go — but thanks, anyway."

Pathetic. Another dance hanging against the wall with James and David, and not even having Ivy there to fantasize about. I was bummed.

That night I decided to go over and see my cousin Roland, the other musician in our family. I hadn't seen him since Christmas, when our families always get together. Roland's mom is my Auntie Bea (she's not my real aunt, she's actually my mom's first cousin) but our families got close since his parents are divorced, too — except he's not *hapa*; both his parents are Asian. Roland's two years older than me. We used to hang around a lot when we were younger, but then when he was a senior and I was a sophomore, he started going with Molly Fletcher. This is a little complicated, but Molly's Asian and her parents are white — she's adopted. Anyway, after Roland and Molly got together I didn't see so much of him — which happens all the time when a guy starts going with someone. Then he went to the U and since then months go by without us seeing each other.

But Roland came to mind after Ivy turned me down for the Spring Thang. James and David have about as much experience with women as I do, so they're no help. It's hard to know who to talk to about girls, when you really want to talk, and not just talk the talk and make up lies. I hoped Roland might have some advice for me, and he's a nice guy, so I knew he wouldn't make me feel like a fool. I decided to drop in on him, act like I was checking out the U for next year, and then casually bring up the subject of women.

I wasn't all weird about college applications like a lot of

people in my class. Going in state was the only thing we could afford, and I figured I'd get into either the U or Western. Ivy had applied for scholarships all over the place. She mostly had her heart set on Howard, which was something I didn't want to think about, since she'd be so far away if she did go there. But she was applying to the U as a backup. I'd feel bad for her if she didn't get into Howard, she wanted it so much, but her backup would be the up-front first choice for Ice Hapa, believe me.

Roland was living in one of the big dorms at the U. Those coed dorms really knock me out. It's a man's paradise. On the way to his room, I saw a beautiful girl coming out of the women's bathroom in her robe. They all live together like that on the same floors and everything. I can't figure out why they all don't flunk out.

I got lucky. Roland was in his room when I got there. He seemed really surprised to see me.

"Rodney — is everything okay?"

"Yeah, Mom's fine, Suzanne's fine, Auntie Bea's fine. I heard Mom talking with her just this morning."

Roland seemed relieved. "So, what're you doing here?" He moved a bunch of clothes off his desk chair for me, then sat on his bed.

"I've applied to the U and to Western and I just thought I'd hang out and see what it'd be like to go here." I sat down and glanced out the window over his desk. "This place is huge."

"Yeah, Western's a lot smaller. More like going away somewhere — to go up to Bellingham."

"Did you go home a lot your first year?"

"Not that much, hardly at all second semester." He laughed. "Mom stopped calling as much then, too." Roland rummaged around a pile of clothes, beer cans, and take-out boxes on the floor next to his bed and came up with a bag of Fritos. "Want some?"

"Thanks," I said, grabbing a handful. "How's Molly?"

"Great — she's got a big paper due next week, so I won't be able to see her until Saturday night. But we're doing good." Roland stuffed another handful of Fritos in his mouth. "These are kind of stale."

"Yeah." I hadn't wanted to mention it, but they were real soggy. "How's the dorm food?"

"Between C - and D +. But probably better than Army food." Roland ate another handful. "How're things going for you?"

"Pretty good." This was an opening to ask him about Ivy, but instead I blew it. I chomped on the chips. "See the M's last night?"

"No. I had to study. How'd they do?"

"Terrible." It seemed easier to talk about baseball than about what was really on my mind, and it took me a while to get to it. I went on and on about the M's and their chances this year. After a while, I looked at my watch—we'd been blabbing about baseball for twenty minutes.

Finally, I just blurted out, "I, uh, wanted to talk to you about a girl."

"Something wrong?" Roland looked serious.

"No. . . nothing like that." I wasn't sure how to explain about me and Ivy. So I just told him, "We're not really involved, but I like her. . . . But I can't get her to think of me as more than a friend." Then I told him the whole story about Ivy and Lavell and Ivy and me.

"Women like a little mystery. Maybe you shouldn't always be so available."

"But she says what she likes about me is that I'm reliable."

"Could you make her jealous?" Roland lay back on his bed, putting his feet up on his desk. "Just a little — ?"

"Wouldn't that make me just like Lavell?" I thought for a while. "Man, a guy just doesn't know how to be with women. If you come on too tough, you're too macho — and they say they want a guy who's sensitive and caring. Well, if you're too sensitive and caring, you're a wimp. It can make you nuts trying to figure out what to be."

"A Mach-Imp." Roland chuckled, liking his little joke. Then he jumped up and did his version of a comedy club bit.

"The Nineties Man," he announced as he grabbed his umbrella from the corner. He swaggered around, holding the umbrella out, then yanked it to him, bending over it like he was a caveman and the umbrella was a cave lady and said in this deep macho voice, "I want you, baby. . . I WANT YOU NOW!"

Then he stood straight and held the umbrella lady away from him at arm's length. His voice was high and sugary. "I despise aggression. Why, I'm the kind of guy that wouldn't even squish a spider. I'll just hold your hand, honey, and later I'll jump in the shower."

Then he talked like the announcer again. "That's it ladies and gentlemen, Mach-Imp. . . The Nineties Man!"

When I left I wasn't sure if I had gotten any advice that would help. . . . *Make Ivy jealous?* I didn't think I'd know how to do that even if I thought it would work, but at least after visiting Roland, I went home cheered up.

CHAPTER SEVEN

When I got back from Roland's, Suzanne was sitting at the kitchen table writing something. I got the milk out of the refrigerator and drank some from the carton.

"Don't do that." Suzanne looked up. "Get a glass."

"It's no big thing." I took another swig and put the carton back.

"I don't want your germs all over the carton."

"My germs are all over the house — you can't escape them, Suzanne. No matter how hard you try, they're everywhere."

Suzanne gave me this disgusted look and then went back to writing. She wrote a few words and then chewed on the end of her pencil, deep in thought.

"What're you writing?" I got a bag of potato chips and sat across from her. They were good — nice and crunchy, not stale like Roland's Fritos.

"Do you have to chew so loud? I can't concentrate."

"So, tell me what you're doing and I'll leave."

"I'm writing poetry, if you must know." She put her pencil down. "A haiku poem."

"That's great. I've memorized one from my language arts book. When Uncle Hideki gets here, I'll say, 'Hi, Uncle Hideki,' then I'll recite the poem:

"Old pond —
and a frog jumps in:
water-sound."

"Just like that, as soon as he walks in the door?"

"Well, maybe I'll wait for the right time. Sort of get on the subject of poetry. It's a famous poem by Matsuo Basho. He's known as the greatest poet of Japan. It was right there in my book. This will blow his mind—he'll be so impressed!"

Suzanne glared at me. "Well, I'm writing original haiku. Which frankly, I think is much more impressive. I even have a pen name, since he's still mad that Jiichan dropped the zu from our name."

"What's your pen name?"

"Hiroko Kobayashi. Sounds perfect, don't you think?" Suzanne picked up the paper with great dignity. "Want to hear it?"

"I dunno." I leaned back in my chair and casually folded my arms behind my head. "Yeah, well—I guess so." Actually, I wasn't sure I did. I was beginning to feel outclassed.

Suzanne cleared her throat. "An untitled poem by Hiroko Kobayashi —"

"How come there's no title?" I sat up and ate another handful of chips.

"That frog thing doesn't have a title," she snapped, "and don't chomp on those chips so loud —"

"Name one person that can eat potato chips without crunching — name just one —"

"Do you want to hear this or don't you?" She put the paper down, getting pissed.

"Yeah — okay."

She picked up the paper, cleared her throat again, and then began reading in a soft voice.

"Cherry trees blossom, crane wings soar
Wind whispers
Autumn fog, the moon of winter
Early spring evolves to summer
Love endures."

I started choking on the potato chips.

"Get a drink of water," Suzanne said in this eat- my-dust-voice, "there's more."

I kept choking while I went to the sink and got a glass of water. As I gulped it down, Suzanne read again.

"Sakura ga saita, tsuru ga tobu
Kaze ga sasayaku
Aki no kiri, fuyu no tsuki
Haru wa natsu ni nari
Ai wa tsuzuku"

"What's that?" I couldn't believe this.

"It's not Polish, stupid." Suzanne looked down at her poem. "It's the Japanese translation."

"How'd you learn that?" A few weeks ago Suzanne knew as much Japanese as I did — *sayonara. . . arigato. . . sushi.*

"I'm working on a whole volume using my pen name. It'll be called *Seeds of Silence* by Hiroko Kobayashi and —"

"How'd you learn those words!" I started choking again.

"Brent translated for me —"

"The white guy!"

"Brent studied Japanese at the U," she said smugly. Then she snapped her notebook shut, gave me a superior smile, stuck her nose in the air, and pranced off to her room.

I'm toast, I thought as I watched her leave. When Uncle Hideki heard her stuff, it would totally blow him away. All I had was three lines about a frog. What if the old guy was so jazzed about Suzanne that he'd decide to give *her* all the money!

I was still depressed about this when James came to pick me up to go to the Spring Thang. It was just going to be the two of us because David's boss at Kentucky Fried Chicken asked him to work. The guy who was on the schedule for tonight was sick so they needed David to take his place; he didn't seem to really mind working instead of going to the dance. It wasn't like he was giving up a night of thrills with wild and wonderful women. I told James since David wasn't going that I thought I'd bag it, too. When you have three guys slouched against the wall it doesn't look totally stupid, but two guys looks weak. Also, with Ivy not going, there didn't seem much point to it. But James got pissed and said we shouldn't blow it off just because David had to work.

Even though we've never discussed it, I think James is like me. Each dance we go to we think that's going to be the one where we get the nerve to move off the wall and ask somebody to dance. He likes Dana Lovelett, but his relationship with her has progressed about as far as mine with Ivy. Just friends. Don't get me wrong, I like friends. It'd be terrible to have no friends. But I'd also like to be a guy women crave, someone they long for, pant for, not just a person who loans pens.

"I've got to leave a little early tonight," James said as we pulled up in front of the school.

"How come?" I slid over to the driver's side and got out. The passenger door on James's car is stuck shut, so you always have to get out on his side.

"Karate tournament tomorrow."

I don't know why this had never even occurred to me before, but right here was one of my two best friends, and he was practically an expert at something Japanese!

"Hey, man, could you show me some karate moves and stuff, and maybe loan me your outfit?"

"*Gi*, it's called a karate *gi*."

"Yeah, well, could I borrow it?" I asked him as we walked in the gym.

We strolled around, very nonchalant. Then we found our spot behind the basketball backboard and slouched against the wall and I told him all about Uncle Hideki. It struck us both funny. James is African American and I'm half Japanese and I've got to learn about this stuff from him. It's like Brent being the one to translate Suzanne's poetry. But James was psyched to do it and said he'd come over after his karate tournament to help me. He's a real friend.

I leaned back against the cold brick and scoped out the dance floor. The band was as terrible as we thought it would be — no keyboard, just a lead guitar, a bass, and a drummer with an amp the size of a lunch bucket. Every few minutes something got screwed up in their sound system and there was a piercing screech, like a fingernail on a blackboard but so loud it killed your ears. People screamed back and it got to be almost part of the act, with the band screeching and people screeching on the next beat like they were singing the chorus to a song. Then I got a huge knot in my stomach—over in the corner I saw this couple. They didn't stop and screech like everyone else, they just kept dancing close, their bodies squishing into each other so it almost looked like one person. Except there was no mistaking that hair, all wild and dark, billowing around the girl's shoulders, with the guy's huge hand holding the back of her head close to his chest. It was Ivy and she was dancing, dancing very close, with none other than Lavell Tyler!

I started swearing under my breath.

"What's wrong, man?" James asked.

I didn't want to tell him. It would make me feel worse. "I'm just sick of coming to these things and never moving off this stupid wall!"

"You could dance with my sister."

"Huh?"

"She's over there" — he pointed to the opposite corner of the gym — "with a bunch of her friends."

I've known Mona Robinson for years, ever since James and I first met in middle school. She's a sophomore and I see her in the halls sometimes—Mona's always real friendly. But I never thought of her as someone to dance with, being a guy's little sister and all. I looked over toward the corner where James was pointing.

"Some of her friends look pretty good," he said.

"Is there one of them you want to dance with?" I asked, like it was no big thing.

"Well-uh, maybe." James hesitated for a minute. "Maybe Maria Garcia—"

"We gotta get off this wall."

"Right. I'll go ask Maria and you ask my sister."

"Okay." Then just as we were about to make our move, that pitiful garage band decided to end the set and take a break.

"You want to wait till they come back?" I asked, wondering who'd lose the nerve first, me or James.

"Sure, okay." We leaned back against the wall and my eyes shot over to Ivy and Lavell. They seemed to be jabbering away, maybe arguing or something, but I couldn't tell. I wondered what was going on with them. I was pretty sure Ivy hadn't lied to me when she said she didn't want to go to the dance. She's not like that; Ivy's a very honest person. She would have told me if she was going with Lavell and not just made up some crap. So he must have dumped Deleisha (it was unthinkable that it'd be the other way around) and then asked Ivy. And it all must have happened pretty fast. Probably Ivy would tell me about it on Monday and then I'd spend the rest of the semester once again listening to "The Adventures of Ivy and Lavell." Pitiful.

Then the pitiful band came back. The guy on the lead guitar fiddled with the lunch-box amp, there was a little screech, and then they started to play.

"Ready?" James asked.

"Anytime, man," I said, and we walked that long walk across the gym to his sister and her friends.

"Who asks first?" I whispered as we were halfway across the floor.

"You ask Mona—then I'll ask Maria."

"Okay. Got it."

"Hi, bro," Mona smiled as James and I went up to them. Then she smiled at me. "Hi, Rodney — how ya doin'?"

"Not bad. Uh — dance?"

"Yeah, sure."

I couldn't believe how easy it was. I put my arm around Mona and we headed to the floor. All these years I'd been stuck to the wall and this was all it took. Incredible! Of course, it was my best friend's sister, but still she was female, and as we started dancing and I looked down at her, she was a female who was looking good.

Just a few feet away from us James was dancing with Maria. All right! We'd really done it! I wanted to give him a high five, but we just shot each other a cool thumbs-up.

Mona and I made fun of the band while we were dancing. We had to shout to each other, it was so loud. It got crazy trying to shout over the band, so we laughed and gave up, and I held her a little closer. And she didn't move away. Nice. Very nice. Then I got very gutsy and maneuvered Mona away from James and Maria. I just kept inching along, guiding her a little farther with each line of the song (if you could call the noise they were making a song).

Then we were over near where Ivy and Lavell were still yakking away. It's not like I deliberately decided to go to the corner where they were — I really did want to dance a little farther away from James and Maria. But I just found myself kind of pulled in the direction of Ivy and Lavell. As we danced by them, I made a joke about the band again and Mona laughed. I don't know really if she heard my joke, but she sure seemed to be having fun, and when she laughed I noticed how she had these dimples and that she looked cute. Very cute. I don't think Ivy saw me, but it made me feel good, anyway. A guy's got his pride.

James had such a great time he decided he didn't have to leave early after all. He started dancing with all his sister's friends. I did, too. It was awesome. After the dance we all decided to get pizza. Maria's father was going to pick them up, since they're sophomores and don't drive, but she called him and he said it would be okay if James and I took them home.

I piled in the backseat with Mona, Freddie Mae Gautier, and Donnalee Rutledge. Maria sat in the front next to James. It was so crowded in the back that Freddie Mae had to sit on my lap. It was a wonderful ride to the Pizza Hut with Freddie Mae's nice warm body right on me and all of us laughing about Screeching Pitifuls, which is what we called the band.

James and I felt like we'd won the lottery, walking into the Hut with four fine ladies. Amazing. They'd been there all the time, just hanging around James's house, and we'd never figured it out till now. Better late than never, I always say!

Then, to top it all off, another great thing happened. My cousin Roland and Molly came into the Hut. They waved to me as they looked around for a table. It felt great to be seen there by Roland in the company of such a bevy of beauties — especially after I had told him all the gory details of my one-sided relationship with Ivy.

I went up to the counter to order and Roland came up next to me. "I told you to make her jealous, man — but I didn't mean to do it with a team." He glanced appreciatively at the table where James was sitting with Mona, Freddie Mae, Donnalee, and Maria. "Looks like the first team, too." Then he laughed and punched me on the shoulder.

I couldn't believe it. Roland actually thought I'd planned all this for Ivy's sake. I gave him a big grin. Who was I to tell him any different?

CHAPTER EIGHT

I felt someone brush against my shoulder. "Hi, Rodney." It was Mona. "That was fun, at the dance." Her voice was sweet and friendly.

"Yeah, it was great." I smiled at her. We were in the hall outside my language arts class, just a few minutes before the bell. Mona was wearing an orange-peachy-colored blouse. Actually, it was coral. I know the precise names of a lot of colors since Mom's an artist. When I was a kid, we had a box of one hundred crayons with names like cobalt blue, burnt sienna, and ultramarine. Mom taught us all the names. Suzanne and I would be coloring, and I wouldn't just say, "Gimme the blue." I'd say, "Gimme the indigo." "Then gimme the scarlet," she'd say. Anyway, that coral was so pretty against Mona's honey nut brown skin. Her dark eyes crinkled up at the corners like James's (except he always wears those Spike Lee glasses), which gives her this happy, sparkly look. And then there were the dimples when she smiled or laughed, which I noticed at the dance. Had Mona always looked this good? Maybe I was the one who needed glasses—real ones, not fake like James's.

We started laughing again about the band. This time I knew

she could hear my jokes. I was doing imitations of Screeching Pitifuls, which were cracking her up, when Ivy walked by us and into the classroom.

"Well, I've got to get to my class." Mona put her hand on my arm. "See you later."

Could she be really thinking of me as somebody other than just one of her brother's friends? I wondered as I went in the room.

Ivy was opening her notebook as I slid into my seat.

"Need a pen?" I asked, feeling quite cheerful.

"No," she snapped, and started rummaging in her purse. I got my book out and read the biography of that guy Matsuo Basho. Maybe that poetry Suzanne was making up was pretty good, but if I knew a bunch of facts about a real Japanese poet, I was sure that would impress Uncle Hideki just as much— maybe more, and I'd still be in the running for the big green.

In the book it said that Matsuo Basho "went to work for a noble family and became the companion of the son. When the son died, Basho was greatly upset. He left the family's service and became a wandering poet, teaching haiku to make a living. One day, according to legend, Basho was out with some students. One of them suddenly announced that he had thought of a poem: 'Pluck off the wings of a bright red dragonfly and there a pepper pod will be.' Basho informed the student that he would never be a poet. A poet, according to Basho, would have created this image: 'Add but the wings to a bright red pepper pod and there a dragonfly will be.' Whether the story is true or not, it reflects the deep compassion for all living things that, along with his superb technical skills as a poet, made Basho a major figure in world literature."

That dragonfly stuff seemed like something I could discuss

with Uncle Hideki. After I read it, I looked over at Ivy. She was still digging in her purse.

"Here." I handed her a pen.

"Thanks," she muttered, grabbing the pen out of my hand, not seeming in the least bit appreciative of my generosity. She sat there slamming her books around, twirling the pen, and generally just fuming under a big cloud of gloom. What was wrong with her, anyway? Rather than just sit there speculating, it occurred to me that I could ask her. Nike. Just do it. So I leaned close to her and put my hand on her arm. "Ivy, what's wrong with you?"

"Nothing." She pulled away. "I don't want to talk about it."

"Fine." No sense in bugging her. I turned to the page in the book where it described haiku.

> . . .*haiku is a highly compressed form of Japanese poetry that creates a brief, clear picture in order to produce an emotional response. Haiku relies heavily on imagery, usually drawn from nature, and on the power of suggestion. When written in Japanese, a haiku poem has three lines of five, seven, and five syllables. When haiku are translated or written in other languages, however, the number of syllables is less important than the mood and imagery of the poem.*

I thought about this as I started writing a little haiku poem about Ivy.

Iv-y seems pis-sed (five syllables)
Her con-ver-sa-tion I miss (seven syllables)

Then I wrote, "*Still wish she's my la-dy*," but that made six syllables, so I crossed it out and changed it to, "*Wish she'd be my girl*."

This poem didn't seem much like haiku, since it wasn't about bugs and frogs and other things in nature, even though it did have the right amount of syllables. But it was exactly how I felt about Ivy. She didn't say another word through the whole class and as soon as the bell rang, I was history — she got up and tore out of there without so much as a glance back at me. Why was she acting mad at me? What did I do? I'm the one who technically should be mad at her. I ask her to the dance, she turns me down, says she's not going because it would be hard for her to see Lavell there with Deleisha, then she shows up at the dance with the dude. And — with not so much as a single explanation to me. I'm *definitely* the one who should be mad.

At lunch, I was going to my locker and I saw Ivy and Lavell. They were huddled in the corner outside the auditorium, only it didn't look like they were just talking — arguing was more like it. He had his arm on her shoulder and she seemed really upset. I got to my locker and I could see them out of the corner of my eye. Maybe I could strut over there and glare at him, hard and mean. "Take your arm off my woman," I'd growl, staring him down. Ivy would look up at me, tears welling up in her huge peanut butter cup eyes. "Oh, Rodney," she'd say, her soft voice brimming with gratitude. Then she'd turn away from him and I'd put my arms around her and we'd leave him in the corner crushed in defeat by a reliable opponent.

I sighed and pulled out my lunch bag. Yuk. It was all greasy. I had put so much mayonnaise on my sandwich it had swished out all over the bag. I walked to the lunchroom, passing Ivy and Lavell and holding the bag away from me so it wouldn't get on my shirt. Maybe after James taught me some karate, I really wouldn't be afraid of messing with a guy as huge and fast as Lavell Tyler. Wouldn't that be something! After all, James helped me get up the confidence to dance with his sister — maybe anything was possible.

My first karate lesson was Saturday. James picked me up after I got through work at the cleaners. When we got to my house and opened the front door, the whole place smelled like a flower store. I couldn't believe it. There were branches from cherry trees all over the place, all stuck in vases with a bunch of other flowers, too.

"Aaaa-chooo!" James sneezed. "Aaaaa-chooo! Aaaaa-chooo!" He started to have a total sneezing fit. "I've got to — AAAA-CHOOO! GET AAACH- OUTA-CHOO-HERE, MAN!"

We tore out of the house, slamming the front door behind us. James was all congested, sniffling, with his eyes getting puffy and starting to water, tears squishing out of them. He sniffed and wiped his nose on his sleeve.

"Wait here, I'll get some Kleenex or something." I went back in the house. Suzanne was in the kitchen, standing at the sink, which was filled with tons of flowers and cherry tree branches.

"What's with the flower store!" I yelled as I grabbed some Kleenex.

"I'm practicing." She looked at a book that was open on the counter next to the sink.

"Practicing what?'

"Ikebana."

"Ike-what?"

"Ikebana. Japanese flower arranging."

"Well, your icky flowers have just arranged to destroy my first karate lesson!" I stomped out and slammed the door.

James was still a mess, leaning against his car sniffling like crazy when I handed him the wad of Kleenex. He opened the driver's door and I got in and slid over. Then he got in.

"I'm allergic," he said, blowing his nose.

"I noticed. Sorry, man."

"Those flowers for your mother's art or something?" he asked.

"No. Suzanne is trying to learn Japanese flower arranging."

"I have to go to my place and take a pill," James sniffled as he put the car in gear.

James was stuffed up all the way to his house. I looked at all the cherry trees in bloom as we drove along Lake Washington Boulevard. Suzanne made me sick. She had that pretty poetry and now these flower things and here I was with my karate master sneezing his head off. At this rate I'd never finance my CD.

Mona and her friend Maria were there when we got to James's house. Seeing Maria seemed to cheer up James enormously. Can't say I minded seeing Mona, either.

"Thought you guys were doing karate at your house?" she asked when James went to take his pill.

I explained what had happened. "It was terrible; it hit him the minute we opened the door."

"Sometimes he can hardly breathe," Mona said sympathetically. "We can't have any flowers in the house."

James came back from the bathroom, blowing his nose.

"I get allergies, too," Maria told him. Then the two of them talked all about their allergies and when they were the worst and what pills helped.

"Want something to drink?" Mona turned to me.

"Sure." I got up and followed her to their kitchen.

"We've got Coke, Squirt" — she opened the refrigerator — "and there's some orange juice."

"Juice. Thanks."

"I saw you signed up for Talent Night," Mona said while she poured the juice. "What're you going to do?"

"Rap."

Mona started to giggle.

"What's so funny?" I gulped the juice.

"It's just a little hard to picture," she said, really laughing now.

"What's so funny in there?" James called from the living room.

I finished my juice and put the glass in the sink. "Did the pill work, man?" I asked as I went into the living room.

"Yeah — want to work on the karate?"

"Right." I followed James down to the basement. Mona and Maria stayed in the living room. I could hear them giggling as we went down the stairs. I remembered how Ivy had acted when I first told her about my being a rapper. Ivy was sweet, a mature person. Giggling seems to be one of the differences between a sophomore girl and a senior.

"Here, put this on." James handed me a white karate outfit. "It's good to practice wearing this, so you get the hang of moving in it."

"This has a white belt. . . ." I noticed as I slipped it on.

"It's my old one, from when I was a beginner."

"How many colors are there?" I tied the belt around my waist.

"In Japan there's just white, brown, and black—although there are degrees of black belt. But in the States they made different levels. After white there's orange or yellow — it depends on the *dojo* —"

"The what?"

"The *dojo*. That's the name for a karate club. And you don't say 'ker-ah-dee' the way you just did — it's kah-rah-tay."

"Karate," I said, trying to pronounce it right. "And what'd you say the name of the outfit is again?"

"*Gi. . .* karate *gi*."

"Karate *gi* ...got it."

"I had a teacher from Japan, so I learned the correct Japanese words for the stances; there's *kiba-dachi, zenkutsu-dachi*, and *nekoashi-dachi*. First we'll try the *kiba-dachi*, or horse stance."

"Okay."

"Oh, I almost forgot, the first thing you do is bow." James gave a little bow and I copied him. "Now bend your knees, put your toes out and spread your legs apart like a bridge." James showed me and I watched him carefully, then tried to place my feet and legs exactly like his.

Then he demonstrated three kicks, a front kick, a side kick, and one he called the roundhouse. He knew the Japanese names for them, too. *Mae-geri, sokuto*, and *mawashi-geri*. It was harder than it seemed. Trying to learn the precise positioning of my body didn't come that easily, since my legs seemed as precise as a couple of rubber bands.

"Good, now move your knee out a little."

"Like this?"

"No—too much, just about a quarter inch the other way." James was calm, but very exact.

"A quarter inch! When I breathe everything moves a quarter of an inch." I wasn't sure I had the patience for this sport.

We practiced for about an hour until it was time for me to go home.

"Thanks, man," I said as James dropped me off in front of my house. "Really appreciate it."

"If you practice a lot, you can probably get a few kicks looking good before your uncle gets here."

James was great. Very encouraging — he even let me keep his karate *gi* to practice with.

When I got home, the house wasn't filled with all those stupid flower arrangements, thank goodness. But then one caught my eye. It was in the middle of the coffee table in the living room. Suzanne had moved all the magazines, books, and mail that are usually piled up there, cluttering the table.

The flowers were placed in the center in a slim, cylindrical vase. I didn't recognize the vase; it was pale gray and the cherry branches stuck out of it in a simple way. The arrangements had balance and harmony (I read somewhere that these were important principles in Japanese design). In any case, they didn't look like they were just stuck in there any old way. Glancing around the room, I saw there weren't any other arrangements. Just that one that looked so perfect — I guess Suzanne had been doing all the other ones for practice. The house still smelled like a flower store, though. I was glad I wasn't allergic.

In the kitchen, I turned on the oven and got the lasagna Mom had made out of the refrigerator. Then I washed and tore up a bunch of lettuce for a salad and put the lasagna in the oven. Suzanne and I usually take turns helping with dinner. I heard the white guy's car drive up and in a few minutes Suzanne came in.

"What's for dinner?" she asked.

"Lasagna."

"Mom's or a frozen one?"

"Mom's."

"Mmm — good." She peeked in the oven.

"What happened to all the flower things?" I got the milk out and took a swig from the carton.

"Rod-ney!"

"What?"

"Get a glass! How many times have I told you —"

"Why does an older sister think she has the right to sound like a mother. . .just tell me that." I put the carton back in the refrigerator.

Suzanne didn't answer me. "So — what happened to the flowers?"

"I was practicing; I finally got one that looked just like the book; it was absolutely perfect."

"That one on the table?" I asked.

"A classic example of ikebana." She smiled her superior smile. "And it should last until he gets here."

I looked in the oven and checked on the lasagna, then I went to my room and put on James's karate *gi*. I stood in front of the mirror trying some of the stances he had showed me. Front stance. . . *zenkutsu-dachi* . . .lookin' good . . .cat stance for sparring. . . *nekoashi-dachi*. . . right, I look great! Then I made a noise he had taught me (it's meant to intimidate the opponent). . . *KIAI!* YES! Front punch. . . front kick. . . *KIAI!*

I was on a roll. . .kick. . . punch. . . *KIAIIIIIII!*

"WHAT'S ALL THIS YELLING!" Suzanne stood in the door to my room, glaring and shouting at me.

I swung my leg around. "It's what you're supposed to do

when — whoops!" My foot slipped and as my leg swung it swept all the junk off my dresser and I flew up and then landed on the floor on my back. Yikes! I lay there flattened, spread-eagled, in the middle of empty Coke cans, my Mariners pennant, a bunch of CDs, and a moldy Kentucky Fried Chicken box. I sat up and threw the chicken box in the corner. Guess I couldn't talk and kick at the same time. I threw a Coke can out of the way.

"What're you doing in here jumping around in that bathrobe!" Suzanne glared down at me.

I got up with as much dignity as possible, rubbing my butt. "It's a karate *gi*," I said, giving her an intimidating stare. I stomped out and went to the living room, which had more space. Suzanne followed me, but I ignored her.

In the living room, I practiced some more kicks. I announced each one in Japanese just to show Suzanne that I knew some stuff, too.

"*Sokuoto.*" I did the side kick.

"*Gyaku-zuki.*" A dynamite front punch.

Then I did the roundhouse kick (I couldn't remember the name in Japanese). It was a tricky one; you had to pivot around. As I was pivoting, Mom came in the front door.

"Whoo — oooooooops!" I lost my concentration. "Yikes!" My leg flew out from under me, then my other leg flew out. "Whooooooops!" On my way to the floor, I creamed the flowers.

"MY FLOWERS!" Suzanne shrieked.

I landed on my butt, drenched with water. Little pink petals were all over the karate *gi* and the cherry blossom branches were strewn across the living room floor. The puddle of water from the vase slowly seeped into the rug.

"YOU'VE DESTROYED MY IKEBANA!" Suzanne screamed, going totally nutso. "Look at this! Look at this mess! YOU BROKE THE VASE, TOO!"

I looked up at Mom, expecting to get double-teamed with her chiming in on the yelling, but she stood frozen in the doorway. She stared at us. Then her nose got red and her eyes were shiny, which is how Mom looks when she starts to cry. I didn't know if it was some special vase of hers that I'd never seen, or if she was upset that Suzanne and I were going at it. But whatever it was, I felt bad. Suzanne turned to Mom, probably about to tell her what a jerk I was but saw that she was upset.

"I'll clean it up — " I mumbled.

Without saying a word, Mom left the living room and went to her bedroom. I looked at Suzanne. "Was the vase hers?"

"No, mine. I got it special."

"Sorry." I crawled around picking up the cherry blossom petals. The little suckers stuck on the rug and it was hard to get them up. Suzanne went to the kitchen and came back with some paper towels. She got down on the floor with me and blotted up the water.

"She's probably mad at both of us for fighting," she said, pressing down on the rug with the paper towel.

"Do you think we should go and talk to her?" I whispered.

"Yeah, as soon as we clean up the mess."

I picked up the broken pieces of the vase and put them in the trash in the kitchen. Then I got the vacuum cleaner while Suzanne wiped the coffee table.

"Sorry about your flowers, Suzanne," I said as I plugged in the vacuum.

"Yeah." She sighed. "Let's just fix this and then see about Mom."

I vacuumed the rug and got up the last of the petals.

"Do you think I should do the whole floor?" I asked.

"No, it looks fine, let's go talk to her."

I put the vacuum away and Suzanne and I went to Mom's room. Her door was shut. We looked at each other and then I knocked.

"Mom?"

No answer.

"Maybe she wants to be alone," I whispered.

"I'll try." Suzanne tapped her knuckles against the door. "Mom?"

Finally the bedroom door opened. Mom's eyes and nose were redder. She was blotting her eyes with a Kleenex.

"The living room's all fixed," I said.

"The mess is gone," Suzanne tried to reassure her.

Mom didn't tell us to leave, so we assumed she meant for us to come in. Suzanne sat on the bed, I flopped down next to her. Mom went to her desk where she had a photo album open and she sat there, staring at one of the pages.

"The cleaners pays me next Saturday — I can get a new vase."

"That's not it."

"You're not upset because I broke Suzanne's vase?"

"The vase is just a thing." Mom sniffed and then she blew her nose. "Things are to be used and people are to be loved, not the other way around."

That's what Mom says automatically whenever Suzanne and I break something — it's a reflex with her, the way some people say, "Bless you," when someone sneezes. The person who used to go completely berserk because you broke something was my dad. Not that Mom liked it if we wrecked stuff, but

I'm pretty sure she started reciting that "people are to be loved" saying when we were little to counteract his temper tantrums.

Being in Mom's room with Suzanne made me think about the time after Dad left. Suzanne must have been about seven, so I would've been five. A lot of mornings Mom would let us crawl in her bed — we'd laugh and horse around and she'd tickle us, which we thought was hilarious. Saturday mornings were the best. She'd drink coffee and read the paper with one of us cuddled on each side of her in our pajamas while we watched cartoons.

Suzanne and I had been close back then. One time when I got a terrible report card and was afraid to show Mom, Suzanne helped me study for my spelling tests every day after school when Mom was at work. She helped me with multiplication tables, too — which I was also lousy at. I glanced over at her, sitting next to me on Mom's bed. It seemed like we'd been in our own worlds for a long time now.

Mom turned a page of the album. "I admit this Uncle Hideki business has stirred up all kinds of things for me." She stared at the photos. "But you kids act like the meaning of the reparations money has nothing to do with anything — it's like you have no clue about it."

"We know about the internment — " Suzanne sat up straighter on Mom's bed.

Mom looked up, her eyes boring into us. "But you both act like getting the money would be the same as winning the lottery!" she snapped. "And you haven't shown the slightest bit of curiosity about what Uncle Hideki is like — that it might be nice to get to know him —"

Suzanne and I both sat there, not knowing what to say. Finally I pointed at the album. "Is that him?"

"No. That's me and Don Kurose." She handed me the album and I shared it with Suzanne.

"Is he a relative?" Suzanne asked. In the photo there was a young man who looked about twenty, wearing a U.S. Army uniform, holding a little girl of about two. They were standing against a barbed wire fence.

Mom came over and sat next to us. "His family lived in the same barracks we did. Actually, we knew them in San Diego —"

"They were sent to Poston, too?"

"To the Santa Anita racetrack first, where they put us before we were sent to the desert in Arizona." Mom pointed to another picture on the same page, a photo of two ladies standing together. "That's Baach and Mrs. Kurose — supposedly she helped deliver me when I was born at the racetrack." Mom turned the page. "Here's another one of their son on leave from the Army. He was in the 442nd."

"Roland's grandfather was in that," I said. "Roland has all his medals."

"He probably has a lot. It was the most highly decorated unit in the Army all Japanese Americans. If you didn't learn this in history, you should have. They were sent out ahead in Italy like cannon fodder — all proving what good Americans they were and then, like Don — coming home on leave to visit their parents — American citizens — imprisoned in camps."

I looked at the picture of Mom and the soldier. Then I looked at my karate *gi*. It was still damp in places and had a few cherry blossoms stuck to it.

"I feel stupid," I mumbled.

"Rodney, the internment camps are at the core of what it means to be Japanese American," Mom said emphatically, although she sounded less angry at us.

"What we're doing is really phony," Suzanne admitted. "But how can camp be at the core of what it means to be Japanese American for our generation? We weren't even born."

"Because the lesson of camp is that race always defines how other people initially react to you — Asian Americans have faces that look 'foreign' and that overshadows how long we've been here or how 'American' we've become."

"You really believe that?" Suzanne seemed upset.

"So you think we should stop doing anything for Uncle Hideki's visit?" I wasn't sure what Mom meant.

"All I'm saying is that what's gotten me upset is your not giving a thought to what the reparations money really means." Mom paused for a minute then closed the album. "I think it's good if Uncle Hideki's visit has sparked some interest in your heritage — but if you have an interest, it should be real."

"Food," I piped up, not having to think about it.

"Huh?" Suzanne looked at me.

"I'm interested in Japanese food."

"I know I don't cook that much —" Mom seemed apologetic.

"I'd like to learn to make miso soup and not from a package — with real tofu." Suzanne was getting into it. Great stuff—we could make that."

Suzanne stood up, she was psyched. "You and I can go shopping and then —"

"Shopping? Why shopping?"

"Food shopping, hot rod."

I smiled. She hadn't called me that since fifth grade.

CHAPTER NINE

"**S**o who's the girl?" Ivy hissed at me.

"Today we're going to discuss Act Four of *Julius Caesar*," Mr. Alexander announced. "What new ironies do you see emerging in this act. Think about the original goal of the conspirators and the attitudes and actions of Antony and Octavius."

"Huh?" I turned to Ivy while I got out my book.

"That girl you were with at the dance?"

"Oh, that girl." I started to tell Ivy it was just James's sister, but then my cousin Roland's words came to me like an oracle from the gods. *Make her jealous.* "Her name's Mo-na." I sighed, drawing out her name so it sounded like a low, sexy moan. I opened my book to Act Four of the play. "So, did you get back together with Lavell?" I tried to sound casual.

"No."

"I thought you weren't going to the dance. . . *Et tu, Brute?*" I mumbled.

"What'd you call me?" Ivy glared at me.

"Nothing. It's from the play."

"I wasn't going. Then he called and said he was through with Deleisha and asked me to go with him."

"All he had to do was beckon —"

"No, Rodney, it wasn't like that!" She was furious. "I only said I'd go to the dance and that was it."

"I've seen you with him lately — " I said accusingly.

"So, I've seen you with that Mona girl!" Ivy snapped.

"Well, are you back together or aren't you?"

"We're not; he's as unreliable as ever." Ivy got out her notebook and I knew she'd want a pen so I just handed her one. "Here."

"Thanks," she growled, then the corners of her beautiful mouth turned up and she smiled, like she didn't want to but couldn't help it.

I laughed first. Then she did, too, also like she couldn't help it. Ivy glanced down at her paper and started doodling with the pen, then she looked over at me. "I have to go downtown this afternoon, want to go with me?"

"Yeah, okay. I guess so. . . oh, wait a minute. I almost forgot. Suzanne and I are going to Uwajimaya. Mom took the bus to work, she let me have the car. This is the weekend Uncle Hideki's coming and we're shopping for a dinner we're going to make for him."

"Oh." Ivy seemed disappointed.

I wished I could figure out how to be two places at once, like the electric grandmother in the story Ivy and I read for our project. This was seriously frustrating.

Mr. Alexander droned on and on and I looked down at the book, when a line from the play jumped out at me. It was where Cassius says to Brutus, "I denied you not." I will deny her not. (If traffic doesn't mess me up.)

"I could meet you downtown when Suzanne and I are through if you want. We should be done by five and I can just take her home and then shoot back downtown."

"Okay. By the espresso cart in front of Nordstrom's — about five-thirty."

After school I picked Suzanne up at the U. She was waiting for me in front of the student union. As I pulled up to the curb, I looked across the campus at Roland's dorm.

"I wish we had time to stop in and see Roland," I said as Suzanne got in.

"We can if you want — " She buckled her seat belt. "I haven't seen him in a while. Sometimes I bump into him at the gym."

"I can't, after we shop I have to go back downtown and get Ivy." I headed off the campus onto 25th.

"Did you see Mom this morning?" Suzanne asked as we came up to a light. "I didn't have any classes until this afternoon, so I slept in. She'd gone to work by the time I got up."

"Yeah, she had coffee while I ate."

"How'd she seem?"

"Better. I think it was good for her to get all that stuff off her chest about the reparations money — oh, man. . . ."

"What's wrong?"

"Montlake Bridge is up. We might be here all day."

"Maybe we should've taken the freeway —"

"It's close to rush hour," I reminded her, "it'll be terrible everywhere."

"So, did she say anything else this morning?"

"Yeah, a lot. It was like she had to keep talking about it. She told me the worst thing for her wasn't camp, since she was born at that racetrack where they first sent them and then was three when they got out, she didn't remember much about it."

"It was after the war, right? When everyone hated them. That's what she always told me the few times she's talked about it."

"Did she tell you about the gang of white boys who'd scream 'Jap' at her — hurling stones and rocks at her going home from school?"

"Makes me want to beat the crap out of someone."

"Did she tell you that part?"

"What part?" The bridge was back down, so I started the engine.

Suzanne didn't say anything.

I drove onto the bridge. "What part?"

"She'd lose control on the way home — she was so terrified, soil herself, is how she put it."

I slammed my fist on the steering wheel.

"Don't swear." Suzanne looked out the window, her voice catching in her throat.

We didn't talk the rest of the way. When we got to the International District, I found a parking space right in front of Uwajimaya. Suzanne and I got out of the car and went into the store. I love Uwajimaya. They have all kinds of things there, not just food, but dishes, books, records, clothes—all kinds of Asian stuff. I was glad we were there so we'd get our minds on the dinner.

"Remember, Mom said 'no chopsticks.' " Suzanne reminded me as we cruised the aisles.

I stopped in front of some chopsticks. "Look at these, they're plastic. We could get these."

"They're Chinese." Suzanne picked up a pair of long maroon plastic sticks.

"I didn't know there was a difference."

"I'm not sure, but I think the Chinese ones are longer."

"Chopsticks would make it more fun, and Mom wouldn't get mad about the trees." Mom was against wood chopsticks; she said it was a terrible waste and totally unnecessary to cut down trees just to make chopsticks.

"Okay." Suzanne counted out four pairs. "These all match, or should we get different colors?"

"Matching is nice. Did you get the recipes?"

Suzanne opened her purse and took out a list. "Here's what we need."

I followed her through the food section and we got all the ingredients. We had trouble finding the *katsuobushi*, which is this sun-dried fish flake stuff for the soup, and the *nori*, which is seaweed, so we had to get a clerk to help us. She also helped us with some stuff that Suzanne's friend Brent said we really should try, since it was traditional and delicious: *natto*, fermented soy beans, and *takuan*, pickled white radish.

"You know that cookbook I got said that gyoza was originally a Chinese dish," Suzanne said while we waited in line.

"David Woo always reminds me that everything was originally Chinese. But if that's true about the gyoza," I said as I took the stuff out of our cart and put it on the check stand, "then it'll go with the plastic Chinese chopsticks."

I looked at my watch. It was four-fifteen. I'd have plenty of time to get Suzanne home and still be back downtown in time to meet Ivy.

We left the parking lot and I took Jackson Street home. It

was a lot faster than messing with the freeway. So far so good. The traffic was okay.

"Just because I called you hot rod doesn't mean you should speed." Suzanne opened the glove compartment.

"I'm not," I said, but I slowed down anyway.

She pulled some tapes out and looked at them. "Don't you have anything but rap?"

"Nope."

I waited for her to say some nasty thing, but she didn't. She just put the tapes back in the glove compartment and turned on the radio.

It was only four-forty when I pulled up in front of our house. Not bad. Suzanne and I each grabbed a grocery sack and carried them into the kitchen.

"You know if this dinner turns out as great as I know it will, we could cook some other times together and invite people over," Suzanne said while we unpacked the groceries.

"That'd be fun." I put the tofu in the refrigerator. "Do you think we should have gotten those little dishes for the *sunomono?*"

"We can just put it on salad plates. Mom said we should only do things that really interest us. Not have stuff to impress him." Suzanne folded her grocery sack. "And I'm not interested in those little dishes."

"I thought the dishes were kind of cute. I liked those soup things, too, with the little tops on them."

"We have soup bowls. They're good enough."

"Okay." I put the cucumbers in the refrigerator. "Well, that's it. I'll see you later."

As I left the kitchen, Suzanne called after me.

"Rodney. . . ."

"Huh?"

"That was fun, thanks." She smiled.

"Yeah, it was. See ya."

As I got into the car it occurred to me that Suzanne can be pretty nice when she wants to, which is probably why she has so many guys after her. Not just because she's good-looking.

I played a tape, classic rap — good old Run DMC, while I drove back downtown. Man, everything was coming up soon. I'd been so focused on the Uncle Hideki thing, that I hadn't been practicing my music as much as I usually do. Talent Night was right around the corner—the great Ice Hapa would have to get busy.

It was five-fifteen when I got downtown. I had some time to kill before I was supposed to meet Ivy so I wandered around Nordstrom's for a while. I wondered what it would be like to have money and just be able to buy anything you wanted. It would change your perspective, probably the stuff wouldn't look as good. For a minute I pretended I could buy anything, but then, just as I thought, I didn't see anything that great. I looked at some pants that seemed to be trying to have a garage sale look, the material was sort of faded and beat up. Eighty dollars. What a rip-off.

I strolled around the main floor, got bored (how can Suzanne shop so much?), and finally decided to position myself at the counter right before the door that led outside to the espresso cart. That way I could see Ivy when she came down the escalator. I was sure glad there hadn't been a lot of traffic. The last thing I'd want to do was show up late and have Ivy think I was not reliable. She makes such a big deal about that.

I wished I could figure out where things were with me and Ivy. She wouldn't go to the Spring Thang with me, but she wasn't back with Lavell, either. Something seemed different about the way she was acting with me, but were we still just friends, or what?

I leaned back against the glass display case and stared at the escalator, imagining Ivy somewhere up in the Brass Plum in a dressing room. I pictured Ivy taking off the jeans and ultramarine sweater she had worn to school, getting into a black, sexy, low-cut dress. . . . I was doing some pretty deep daydreaming....Ivy in her underwear. . . Ivy pulling a dress over her head. . . I closed my eyes, picturing every detail of Ivy in that dressing room. . . .

"Excuse me!" snapped this shrill voice.

I opened my eyes.

"Excuse me!" The voice got louder.

Then I felt this shove and there's this totally pissed old white lady trying to shove me aside so she can see the stuff in the case I'm leaning on. I had been lost in my dreams of Ivy because I wasn't sure how long that lady had even been standing there.

"WHY DON'T YOU GO BACK TO JAPAN!" she shouted in disgust. Then she turned away, muttering to people passing in the aisle, "They think they own everything. . . cars, televisions. . . the baseball team. . . next it'll be the Space Needle for God's sake. . . ."

I froze and just stared at her as she disappeared into the crowd. Then Ivy came up to me. I must have missed seeing her ride down the escalator.

She put her hand on my arm. "Rodney?"

"Huh?"

"Are you okay?"

"I think I just got bashed."

"What?" Ivy looked confused. I stood there, a bit stunned.

"Come on, let's go."

I looked in the crowd, trying to see where the lady had gone. "Rodney?"

"Huh?" I couldn't see her anywhere. She'd just disappeared. I wondered if she had been a daydream, too. I mean a day-nightmare — or maybe she was a ghost. . . this monstrous apparition. . . . like Caesar's ghost. . . .

"Why don't we get a Coke?" Ivy had her hand on my arm. I looked down at her, into her beautiful dark eyes, and began to forget the old lady.

"I promised Mom and Suzanne I'd help clean the house since Uncle Hideki's coming tomorrow."

"I'll help you if you want. I'd like to meet your uncle, too."

I couldn't believe it. Ivy was going to come over and we didn't even have a school project. "Are you sure — I mean —"

"Of course; you've talked so much about him."

"I mean about cleaning."

"I don't mind." She hesitated. "Unless you don't want me to. . . ."

"Ivy. . . I want you to come over."

When we got to my house, Suzanne and Mom had already started cleaning. Mom was scrubbing the woodwork in the living room and we heard water running in the bathroom. It sounded like Suzanne was working on the tub.

"Hi, you're just in time," Mom said, squeezing out a big sponge in a bucket. She smiled at Ivy. "Another project?"

"Hi, Mrs. Suyama. No, I'm just hanging out. I told Rodney I'd help you guys get ready for your uncle."

"I'm ready for a break. Why don't you have a Coke or something, then you can help Rodney attack his room. It's either that or call the health department." Mom carried the bucket into the kitchen and dumped it into the sink. "This water's filthy. I had no idea the woodwork had gotten this bad!"

"It's so gray in Seattle, it makes everything look gray." Ivy laughed. "You never think it's really dirt."

Mom washed her hands and took a big bottle of Talking Rain from the refrigerator, then reached for a glass in the cupboard. "Want some?"

I looked in the refrigerator. "We've got Coke, juice. . . "

"Coke, thanks."

I got Cokes for Ivy and me and we sat at the kitchen table.

"Suzanne, ready for a break?" Mom called as she joined us at the table.

"In a minute," Suzanne yelled from the bathroom. "Hi, Ivy."

"Hi!" Ivy called back.

"Notice she didn't say 'hi' to me."

Suzanne came in the kitchen. "Rodney, I don't believe that shaving cream stuck to the mirror. It's all gunked up in the corners like glue!" She got some juice from the refrigerator.

"Think what great exercise scrubbing is — all the energy it takes. It's a known fact that you burn two hundred and seven calories every twenty minutes when you scrub off stuck shaving cream."

"It's a known fact that with one more crack like that, you'll get bashed with the scrub brush." Suzanne thought this was hilarious.

"I've had my quota for today, actually."

Ivy sipped her Coke. "Are you talking about what happened at Nordstrom's? You looked like you saw something really weird —"

"I did. There was this weird lady. . . . "

"Must have been pretty freaky, the way you looked when I got there."

I took a swig of my Coke, and then I told them about what had happened (leaving out the part about me daydreaming about Ivy in her underwear).

"What did you do after she said to go back to Japan?" Mom looked upset.

"Yeah, what did you say, Rodney?" Ivy chimed in.

"I said, 'My family's been here for three generations —why don't you go back under your rock, you blue-headed old bag.'"

"Rodney!" Mom was shocked, but she also laughed.

"Did you really say that?" Ivy was skeptical.

"No." I sighed. "She stomped off before I knew what happened."

"Nothing like that's ever happened to me." Suzanne sat at the table with us. "I don't know what I'd say."

"You've never heard a racist thing in your life?" Ivy seemed surprised.

"I've had people assume I don't speak English. And in the seventh grade some girl called me a 'chink,' but never that out-and-out bashing."

Mom sipped her water. "I'm sure I probably sound cynical—but I think it's more than just Asian faces being seen as foreign. They're also associated with an enemy."

"You sound a little paranoid, Mom." Suzanne got up and refilled her glass. "I know your generation had a whole different experience, in camp and all but *enemy?* Isn't that a bit much?"

"Okay, just think about it." Mom stood up and went to the sink and squirted soap in the bucket. "In World War II we fought against the Japanese, right after that was the Korean War, the North Koreans were the enemy, then the Communist Chinese were the enemy, and not long after that there was the Vietnam War. The North Vietnamese were the enemy." Mom turned on the faucet and watched the bucket fill up with soapy water. "And now Japan is seen as an economic enemy."

Suzanne looked surprised. "You really believe that?"

"She's right. Our country's had all these wars with people who look like us." I agreed with Mom.

"I think the American people deserve more credit." Suzanne argued. "I mean, no one likes Japan bashing, but I don't think it's that big of a deal."

"Tell that to Vincent Chin's family." I said. Suzanne looked at me like she wasn't sure who I was talking about. "He's the Chinese guy that those auto workers beat to death in Detroit because they thought he was Japanese."

Suzanne began to get triple-teamed because Ivy jumped in. "I agree with your mom," she said. "There're people who can't do anything but hate. Like in Europe — that guy in Bosnia throwing the people in camps. People thought there'd never be anything like that again. Ethnic cleansing — it's the same as with the Jews."

"I can see I'm in the minority in this family. You're all so pessimistic." Suzanne took her glass to the sink and rinsed it out.

"I didn't say there was no hope," Mom said as she carried the bucket to the living room, soap slopping over its sides. "Uh-oh, I filled this too full." She wiped up the suds from the floor. "I just think I'm realistic about racism not going away any day soon."

"I've got to get back to that grungy bathroom." Suzanne grabbed the cleaning stuff and then stopped and looked at her sponge. "I'm going to need another one. This is falling apart from scrubbing so hard." As she left, she glared at me. "And in the future DON'T splatter the shaving cream so much, Rodney!"

"Two hundred and seven calories," I called after her.

Ivy and I got up from the table and all of a sudden I had this great idea. I couldn't help grinning just thinking about it. "I'm gonna do it," I mumbled.

"Do what? Did I miss something here?" Ivy cocked her head looking at me like I was weird.

I grinned some more. "I'm gonna do a rap about bashing." Then I looked at Ivy. ZAM! Another great idea. "Ivy, why don't you be in the act with me. . . for Talent Night."

"I can't do a beat box. I'd just end up spitting on the mike. Besides, I thought you had a drum machine."

"I do, I do." I was getting excited. "See, what you could do is be like that pink Energizer rabbit from those TV commercials. I'll be doing the rap and you'll go back and forth with this bass drum wearing a pink rabbit outfit."

"Rodney, I did not raise you to want to put a young woman in a bunny suit!" Mom yelled from the living room.

"Not a bunny, that rabbit, that rabbit on TV."

"I have pink sweats and I could make some cute pink ears. . . ." Ivy was getting interested.

"Yeah, and you'll go back and forth, and on the drum on one side there'll be the Rising Sun, the Japanese flag, and you'll hit it with a big steel hammer."

"A mallet," Mom chimed in, coming back into the kitchen.

"No, because the steel hammer is bashing Japan, then when Ivy turns around and comes back across the stage, the other side of the drum will have the picture of the earth with a rainbow around it and she'll hit that with a regular bass drum mallet."

Ivy got excited. "Then you'll be doing the rap the whole time while I'm this visual thing!"

"Visual. . .political. . . this is quite an idea, Rodney." Mom was definitely getting into it, like I'm her hope for her politics.

"We just need to perform in front of people before Talent Night," Ivy said, "because we have got to be good."

"You can." Mom rinsed and dried her hands and went through the pile of mail by the kitchen phone. "Look, this came yesterday — I'm glad I didn't throw it out." She handed us a flyer. An *Evening of Community Music at AAP*, it read on the front.

AAP is the Asian American Performers. Mom sometimes goes to plays there. "It's a musical talent show kind of thing, anyone can be in it, and there's still time to sign up," she said, pointing to the entry form.

Ivy and I held the entry form between us and read over it, our heads very close together, which I liked very much.

"Want to do it?" Ivy looked at me with her big dark peanut butter cup eyes.

"Is the Pope Catholic?" I grinned.

Did I wanna do it? Talk. . . dance. . . rap. . . anything, every-thing. . . everyTHING. . . EVERYTHING. . . with Ivy. . . YES! KIAI!

CHAPTER TEN

Suzanne and I stood at the front window of the living room peeking around the drapes as the car drove up. It was six o'clock. The spring days were longer and it was still bright from the gold light of the late afternoon sun. A breeze rustled the branches of the small plum tree in our front yard. I had mowed the grass that afternoon and everything looked pretty tidy, I thought, as I watched the car park in front of the house. I looked at my watch. He was an hour late, his plane must have been held up. He probably came straight from the airport instead of going first to the house of that person on the Cherry Blossom Festival Committee where he said he was staying. At Mr. and Mrs. Hasegawa's or somebody like that in Bellevue.

We'd worked all afternoon on our wonderful dinner. The miso soup was simmering on the stove, the cucumbers were nicely peeled, sliced, and sitting in the refrigerator with the California roll sushi. We decided we'd put the rice vinegar on the cucumbers at the last minute; we also had some nice little shrimp to plunk on top of them. Actually, we made all the rest of the stuff ahead of time, too. You're really supposed to cook the shabu-shabu at the table, but Suzanne and I thought we might get extremely nervous trying to cook the food right there in front of Uncle Hideki's face. So we went ahead and cooked the shabu-shabu on the stove and just put the pot in the oven with the temperature set on "warm." Then we browned the gyoza in the deep fryer. They were all cooked and ready to just pop in the microwave to be heated up. We were set! What a feast it would be!

"He looks a little like Jiichan," Suzanne whispered as we watched an old man slowly climb out of the car.

"He's bald, though," I whispered. "Jiichan had more hair."

Mom came in the living room. "Is he here?" she asked nervously.

"Yes. He's getting out of the car," I said.

"Now he's getting out his suitcase," Suzanne reported.

"Now he's walking up the walk," I said quietly.

"You two sound like color commentators whispering at a golf tournament." Mom laughed.

Then we heard the doorbell. Suzanne and I backed away from behind the drapes as Mom went to the door.

"Ojichan, hello," Mom said as she opened the door.

Suzanne and I stood behind her. "How come she called him Grampa?" I whispered.

"No, she said, 'Uncle.'" Suzanne whispered. "It just kind of sounds the same."

"Hello, Helen," Uncle Hideki said. "I apologize for being late."

"It's quite all right, I'm glad you made it." They smiled, but they didn't hug or anything. They didn't touch, didn't even shake hands.

"Hi, Uncle Hideki," Suzanne said sweetly. She went to him with her hand held out and they shook hands. "I'm Suzanne."

"How do you do?" he said rather formally.

"Hi, Uncle Hideki. I'm Rodney, nice to meetcha." I gave him a firm handshake. He was wearing a sport coat, tie, and some dark slacks. Suzanne and I weren't totally slobs, but we had dressed more on the casual side. She had on pants and a silk blouse, and I was wearing khakis and a dress shirt. Mom wasn't that dressed up, either. I started to worry that maybe we should have worn better stuff.

"Pleased to meet you, Rodney."

"Please come in, Ojichan." Mom sounded so nervous, it made me nervous.

"My suitcase?"

"Oh, Rodney, why don't you take it. We can just leave it here by the front door."

I grabbed his bag. "Here, Uncle. . . ."

"Wait, please." The guy wouldn't let go of the bag.

"Uh, sorry." I dropped my hand. Maybe he didn't want anybody to touch it.

He put the bag on the chair in the hall, opened it, and took out a slim cardboard box with a pretty design on it. Then he snapped the bag shut and set it by the door. "Should I set it here? I don't like to leave things in the car."

"Sure, that's fine, Ojichan, Please come in."

Uncle Hideki followed Mom into the living room. "For you, Helen," he said, handing her the box.

"Thank you so much, you shouldn't have. . . ."

We all stood there in the middle of the living room. Suzanne and I glanced at each other. We didn't think we should sit down until he did.

"It's nothing," Uncle Hideki mumbled.

Mom had told me about this, that people from Japan may knock themselves out to make something for you or select a wonderful gift and when you thank them they always say it's nothing and tell you how crummy it is. Even though Uncle Hideki had been in America a long time, he certainly seemed Japanese the way he had that gift part down.

"Uh, please sit down. . . ." Mom opened the box while we all sat down. "Oh, would you like to use the bathroom?"

Uncle Hideki nodded and stood up, so we jumped up.

"Rodney, please show Uncle Hideki." Mom looked inside the box. "*Manju*, how kind of you, Ojichan."

"It's hardly anything," he mumbled. "Nothing at all."

"Right this way, Uncle Hideki," I said as I left the living room with him following me. "It's the door at the end of the hall."

I went back into the living room. "What's *manju?*" I whispered.

"A treat. Something like a pastry," Mom said. She put the box on the coffee table. I hadn't noticed before, but she had brought out her old photo album from when she was a little kid, the one she usually kept in her room. It was on the coffee table, and she put the box of the *manju* stuff from Uncle Hideki next to it.

"Should we eat it now?" Suzanne wanted to know.

"We'll wait till after dinner."

"How come we've never had it?" I asked.

"It's not my favorite," Mom whispered, "but you should try it. You kids might like it."

Uncle Hideki came back into the living room. Suzanne and

I stood up when he entered the room, then we sat down when he did. I was beginning to feel like a jack-in-the-box.

We all sat there, not saying a word. Then finally, Mom said, "Well, Ojichan, when does the Shodo Exhibition begin?"

"Saturday."

"Oh, that's nice." Mom didn't seem to know what to say after that.

Silence.

Then she said, "What time on Saturday?"

"One o'clock."

"Oh."

More silence.

"And you're staying with the Hasegawas in Bellevue?" Mom asked.

"Yes."

More silence. Trying to get Uncle Hideki to talk was like pulling teeth. I decided to try a little sports talk. "Are you a Lakers fan, Uncle Hideki?"

"Yes."

"That's nice. But they're not like they were in the good old days with Magic and Kareem."

"You could say that," he said.

We sat there some more, not saying anything.

More silence.

Then Uncle Hideki looked at Suzanne, then at me. "They don't look *hapa*," he said to Mom right in front of us. Even though his tone wasn't mean, I thought this was pretty rude, especially since he wanted to retain so much of his Japanese heritage and I thought part of that was being polite.

"Well, we have to check on the food. Come on, Rodney." Suzanne stood up.

"Rodney and Suzanne are the cooks tonight and the dinner will be ready in a few minutes."

"Oh, you're not cooking, Helen?" Uncle Hideki seemed surprised.

"The kids wanted to." Mom sounded a little defensive.

I stood up and followed Suzanne into the kitchen. "Not much of a talker," I whispered as I got the sushi out of the refrigerator.

"What a guy." Suzanne got the chopsticks and some napkins and I put the sushi on the plates. We had bought our favorite kind. "Did you notice Mom's album?" Suzanne counted out the napkins.

"Yeah, on the coffee table; looks like she wants to reminisce about the family."

"I suppose so, he's all she's got left on her dad's side." We each got two plates and took the sushi into the living room.

"Have some sushi, Uncle Hideki." Suzanne smiled as she handed him a plate.

Uncle Hideki took the plate. "Thank you," he said as he picked up the chopsticks and held them out in front of him. "These aren't Japanese, you know," he said.

"They're Chinese," I piped up. "Mom doesn't want wood ones."

"It's because of the environment. She doesn't think trees should be cut down to make chopsticks."

Uncle Hideki looked at the sushi and poked it with his chopstick.

"It's California roll—we just love it." Suzanne took a bite of hers. "Rodney and I got them at Uwajimaya."

"Did you know it wasn't authentic?" he instructed us as he popped it in his mouth.

"No, we didn't," I said. "But we think they taste great."

"Did you have a nice flight, Uncle Hideki?" Mom asked him.

"Not really."

Suzanne and I looked at each other and chewed our California rolls.

"That's too bad," Mom said. Then nobody said anything. "Was it crowded?" she finally asked.

"Too crowded. Terrible food." He scarfed down his California roll. "It was late." Then he looked at us. "They're both almost grown, I see."

"Yes, Rodney's seventeen and Suzanne is nineteen."

"Would you like another California roll. Uncle Hideki?" Suzanne asked.

"Oh, no — thank you."

"Have another, Ojichan," Mom said, shoving another sushi at him.

"Oh, no."

"Just one more — " Mom kept pushing it at him. Then I remembered that she said that people from Japan always say "no" and refuse what you give them. This is very confusing to me because I can't figure out when you know they really mean "no" and when they're just going through the motions because they're supposed to say "no" but they really want the stuff. Mom seemed to be able to figure it out, though, I guess, because she had been around enough first generation Japanese Americans like her parents and Uncle Hideki to get how it works. With me, if a person said "no," I'd figure they meant it and that'd be it.

Uncle Hideki gobbled another California roll. For a guy who said it wasn't authentic, he sure seemed to like eating it.

"What do you do?" he asked Suzanne.

"I'm at the University of Washington."

"What are you studying?"

"I'd like to major in business," Suzanne told him.

"And you?" He looked at me.

"I'm a senior in high school."

"What are your interests?" he asked. This was getting deadly. I felt like it was a job interview.

"Music," I said, then I looked at Suzanne. "Maybe we better see about the food."

As Suzanne and I went to the kitchen, the doorbell rang.

"Oh, I bet it's Ivy. I'll get it." We had planned that Ivy would come over after we'd had dinner to meet Uncle Hideki, but I forgot to call her and tell her his plane had been late.

I went to the door and opened it. Yes! It was Ivy — what a beautiful sight! Maybe she'd spark the party and lighten things up a bit because this dinner needed some serious help.

"Hi," I whispered. "I'm really glad to see you. He just got here, his plane was late. Sorry I didn't call."

"Oh, should I come back later?"

Mom came to the door. She seemed relieved, too. "Come on in, Ivy," Mom said. "Have you eaten, honey?"

"Well, no, actually I haven't."

"Then you can have some with us."

We went into the living room and Mom introduced Ivy to Uncle Hideki, who just sat there still gobbling California rolls.

He seemed to grunt "hello," but that was about it. He didn't get up to shake hands.

"Come on in, everybody, and have some soup." Suzanne stuck her head into the living room.

We don't have a dining room, but Suzanne and I had fixed the kitchen table up. It had a nice tablecloth and we had bought some tulips, which we put in the middle of the table in a little vase. It looked pretty good for our old kitchen table.

I set another place for Ivy while Suzanne got another bowl. Everyone sat at the table and Suzanne took the lid off the pot that held the miso soup.

"It's too bad when Japanese culture has been lost to the younger generation," Uncle Hideki said to Mom, looking at the Chinese plastic chopsticks as he picked them up.

"Something's wrong. . . ." Suzanne whispered, looking at the soup.

I looked at the pot while Ivy and Mom and Uncle Hideki sat silently at the table. Uncle Hideki looked at Ivy, then at Mom.

"*Kuronbo*," he said, assuming no one would know what he said except Mom, and he was right. But whatever it was, Mom turned bright red, and she looked like she was going to explode.

"It's all gluey!" Suzanne hissed. "It must have overcooked. The tofu got weird."

"Dump it in the bowls, anyway," I whispered. "Maybe it will taste good."

Suzanne carried the pot to the table and I ladled out the soup.

"Miso soup!" she said cheerfully.

"This is very unusual miso soup." Uncle Hideki peered in the bowl.

"Maybe it'll taste good," Ivy said sweetly, stirring the goop with her chopstick.

Uncle Hideki stared at Ivy. She picked up her bowl and sipped the soup. "I think it's very nice, kind of like split pea."

Then I took the sliced cucumbers and the shrimp out of the refrigerator and shook the rice vinegar on them. Suzanne put the microwave on to warm up the gyoza, but then I started smelling something funny. I kept nervously shaking the vinegar, forgetting I was doing it, and then I realized the cucumbers were drowning in it. "Whoops." I dumped out some of the vinegar and put the plates on the table.

"*Sunomono*," I announced, then I peeked in the oven. Yuk. The shabu-shabu was sitting there smoking. . . a burned-up mess! We must have turned the oven up high by mistake, instead of just leaving it on "warm." We got some potholders and yanked it out of the oven. Mom was still furious. She hadn't said a thing, but she was glaring at Uncle Hideki and I wondered what that word meant that he had said. Ivy acted like she didn't care about whatever was going on, she was the only one eating.

"The shabu-shabu seems to have burned," Suzanne said apologetically. "I can throw together a salad or something."

"Don't trouble yourself, I've got a big day tomorrow." Uncle Hideki jumped up like he couldn't stand being with us another second. "I really must be on my way."

"Gee, you just got here." Suzanne was upset.

"It was nice to meet you, Suzanne." Uncle Hideki took the car keys out of his pocket, jiggling them impatiently.

"And Rodney." He held out his hand, so I shook it.

Then he turned to Mom, reciting his good-bye in a flat voice like he didn't mean a word of it. "Helen, nice seeing you again."

Mom mumbled something and got up and followed him to the door. She looked like she'd rather throw something at him, but forced herself to see him out instead.

"Where's everybody going?" Ivy asked as the kitchen emptied out.

Suzanne and I watched him get in his car. "What's that word he said?" I asked Mom.

"*Kuronbo*," she said, disgusted.

"What's that?" Suzanne asked.

"It means 'black' and it's derogatory." Mom was really upset.

That did it. I charged out of the house as he was pulling away.

"We're the *SUYAMA* family and we care about each other! For all your tradition — you don't have anybody!" I yelled after his car, hoping he had the window down. "Give your money to that sumo fat guy, you old fart!"

When I went back in the house, Mom, Suzanne, and Ivy were in the kitchen beginning to clean up the disaster.

"What a guy," Suzanne said.

"A real prince." I started carrying the plates to the sink. "It's good he never got that sword, he didn't deserve it."

Mom was scrubbing the pan with the burned-up shabu-shabu. Her teeth were clenched and she scrubbed like she wanted to kill the pan.

"Mom, just sit down," I took the pan away from her. "This was Suzanne's and my deal."

"You, too, Ivy." Suzanne grabbed the dish towel from Ivy and Mom and Ivy sat at the table.

"How dare he come in my home and insult our friend!" Mom spat out the words.

"He was as bad as that old basher in Nord-strom's," I said, scrubbing the pan where Mom had left off.

"They'd make a great pair!" Ivy laughed. She was the least upset of anybody and it wasn't because she didn't know what had gone down. Ivy just handles stuff, she's amazing. But Mom didn't smile, she was still furious.

"Maybe we should have ordered out Chinese," Suzanne said, looking at the mess in the sink.

"I liked the soup," Ivy said, "I like split pea."

"Uncle Hideous has no culinary imagination," Suzanne said, and then she and I started singing our Japanese song.

"*Toy. . . o. . . ta . . . Nis. . . san. . . Hon. . . da.* " We belted it out.

Ivy thought it was hysterical, which inspired me toward more Japanese creativity. "Old toad leaves town. . . much happiness." I said, making up a nice haiku poem.

"Let's have some traditional, authentic Italian fast food," Mom said, lightening up, "with an emphasis on the fast."

"Got it." I went to the phone and called Domino's.

While we ate the pizza we were all trying to figure out what to do with the rest of the evening. since things hadn't turned out the way we planned. Mom and Suzanne finally decided to get a video, and Ivy wanted to stay and rehearse our rap act. We had already been practicing getting ready for our first gig at AAP, but she still thought it would be good to get in another rehearsal.

Ivy had the whole thing down, she even moved exactly that robot way the rabbit did on TV. But that was where the comparison left off. Ivy did not look goofy like that rabbit. In her pink sweats she looked sexy. Very sexy. I really didn't think we needed another practice, but Ivy insisted.

"You know, Rodney," she said after we'd run through it for a half hour, "that disaster with your uncle didn't take away any of our energy. We're like real pros! The show goes on! Just think. . . this week AAP, next week. . . FRANKLIN, next month. . . HOLLYWOOD, then LONDON! TOKYO! THE WORLD!"

Ivy had big plans for us.

CHAPTER ELEVEN

"Y ou look great," I told Ivy as she got in the car in her rabbit outfit. "They're going to love us."

"I'm nervous. I brought my coat to put over this for when we go in the theater."

"Good idea, we want it to be a surprise."

I parked in the lot next to the theater and Ivy and I went in. We were scheduled to be the fourth act and there wasn't enough room backstage for the performers, so we all were supposed to sit right in the theater with the audience.

I followed Ivy down the side aisle to the front row, which had been roped off for us. Ivy pulled her coat close around her and kept holding it tight as we sat down at the end of the row. We recognized a lot of kids from school and whispered "hi" to them. But no one talked much; I think everyone there was too nervous. I looked at my watch. It was supposed to start in a few minutes. I looked around the audience. There wasn't an empty seat in the place. Mom and Suzanne were in the back row on the right side. They gave me a little wave.

Then the lights dimmed and a spotlight lit up the center aisle as Phillip Omori, who is the weather guy on KORO, loped down the aisle from the back of the theater and bounded up onto the stage. Everyone clapped.

"Welcome to An Evening of Community Music at AAP!" Everyone clapped again, and he waited until the place had quieted down, then he said, "For our first act we are proud to present a very talented member of the Asian community, Eric Lew, who will play Max Reger's Cello Suite Number One."

His parents probably gave him a cello in his crib, I thought as I listened to him play. The guy was unbelievable. The audience must have clapped for five minutes. Then the emcee came back.

"Ladies and gentlemen, our next performer is Julie Muramoto, who will play Paganini's Caprice Number Twenty-four."

Julie, who looks like a little like Kristi Yamaguchi, got up there with her violin and blew everybody away. She was amazing, like some symphony person.

"Maybe we didn't read the flyer right," I whispered to Ivy, who was fiddling with her bunny ears in her lap. "Maybe it's supposed to only be classical stuff."

"Shhh," she hissed. "We're going to be great. Chill, Rodney."

They clapped for Julie Muramoto for at least five minutes, too.

"Next we have Marlene Santos singing an aria from Verdi's *La Forza del Destino*, 'Pace, pace, mio dio,' " said the weather guy. "Ms. Santos will be accompanied by Martin Wong on the piano."

The audience went wild when that girl finished singing. Then she and Martin Wong bowed, and she left the stage while he stood by the piano. The emcee got up and announced that Martin Wong would play Chopin's "Revolution Etude."

When the audience finally got through clapping for Martin Wong, which seemed like a bazillion years later, the emcee got up on the stage and said, "Ladies and gentlemen, we are happy to present Ice Hapa."

"That's us," I whispered to Ivy.

"Okay, go for it." Ivy kept her coat on and we left our seats and went up on the stage. My drum box was backstage. We both went back there and Ivy took off her coat and put on her ears. I plugged in my drum box and brought it out and pushed back the piano. The lights dimmed. I started to rap:

"Don't be a dope/when we gotta have hope/here's the word, you nerds/don't thrash, don't bash, get along"

Ivy came out in the rabbit suit banging the drum with the Rising Sun on it. There was a big murmur from the audience when they saw her, and Ivy strutted along, her head held high. She got to the edge of the stage and turned, starting back across with the rainbow earth thing facing the audience. I kept rappin'.

"Don't mess the earth/you gotta love this planet! don't break it, we can make it/get along Don't blame, it's a shame/be a friend, we can mend. . . ."

Then Ivy tripped over the cord to my drum box. SPLAT! She landed on her butt, knocking the mike over; the bass drum flew through the air and hit me in the stomach. BAM! Ice Hapa lies flattened with the rabbit. The audience goes berserk, they laugh like maniacs, they are rolling in the aisles. The curtain closes.

Ivy and I just sat on the stage. I wanted to hide there until all the people had left the theater, but then a whole bunch of people came up on stage and burst through the curtain. The Franklin kids were begging us to do the act for Talent Night.

"You were hilarious, Rodney," said Marlene Santos.

"I didn't quite get the rabbit part," Eric Lew said, "but you were funny."

"That was the funniest thing I've ever seen," said Julie Muramoto.

"How come you were selling batteries?" Eric asked.

"It was a commercial for peace, stupid," Jenny Chung chimed in. "One side of the drum showed Japan bashing and the other showed a better alternative, beating the drum for world peace, like we're all on the planet together with the rainbow for harmony and everything, right, Ivy?"

Jenny Chung is a know-it-all and usually gets on everyone's nerves, but Ivy beamed at her. "You got that right!"

"I thought it was about batteries," Eric muttered.

"Great act, you two," Julie said. "You *have* to do it for Talent Night!"

I was still stunned, and I think Ivy was, too. People hung around us while I got my drum box and all the way to the parking lot while Ivy and I carried our stuff to the car. They kept going on and on about how great we were. It was amazing. Then people gradually got in their cars and drove away. I put the keys in the ignition, but then I just sat there.

"What's the matter, Rodney?"

"I was supposed to be cool."

"So, no one has to know that."

"Yeah, but we know."

"At Talent Night, I'll trip on purpose."

"Ivy, you don't seem to get it." I put my head back on the

seat and sighed. "I wanted to be this totally cool rap artist. I wanted to be great."

"We'll change your name, too," Ivy said, ignoring me.

"To what?" I snapped.

"Butterscotch Nut."

"You've got to be kidding!"

Then Ivy snuggled next to me. "It's good making people laugh, Rodney. I like going out with an entertainer."

"But, Ivy, I — "Then she kissed me, and I completely forgot what I was going to say.

After a minute she pulled away and whispered, "You keep being reliable, you hear what I'm saying, Rodney?"

"Uh-huh."

Then I kissed her and we stayed in the car in the dark parking lot for a long time, and I realized that even though Ivy and I had kissed before, this time there was something very different.

This time, Lavell Tyler was nowhere in sight.

EPILOGUE

It was May. The blossoms were all off the cherry trees, and the trees now had their new young leaves. The rhododendrons and azaleas were in full bloom and it was the most beautiful spring I'd ever seen. I suppose that had a lot to do with me and Ivy. The only bad thing about our relationship was that we didn't have a lot of time left together. Ivy had gotten a full scholarship to Howard and I had decided on Western and would be going to Bellingham in the fall and we'd be thousands of miles apart.

Talent Night had been a huge success. It was different trying to be funny as opposed to being funny by accident; but Ivy had us practicing every night the week between our gig at AAP and Talent Night. She even had us rent every movie Steve Martin ever made, since she thought he was a good model of someone who looked ridiculous while trying to be cool, which is what she thought we should aim for in our act. We must have pulled it off, because we were surrounded by our friends after the show, just like we had been after the AAP gig, only this time we even had people coming up and congratulating us who we didn't know.

It was a funny thing about Talent Night. It had been my dream to be this famous rap artist, and even though Ivy and I did our political comedy act instead — which went over big — it ended up that what really mattered to me was all the stuff that happened on the way to Talent Night, not Talent Night itself. Uncle Hideki (we now always refer to him as Uncle Hideous) had made me think about my Japanese half; Mom, Suzanne, and I got a lot closer with Mom talking to us about camp and other stuff she never had before; and the rap ended up in a goofy way being about Japan bashing and people getting along. Speaking of which, it was one of the best things that happened on the way to Talent Night: me and Ivy getting along. I love that girl.

Tonight was the Senior Prom. James would be picking me up around six and then we'd get Ivy and Maria. He had been seeing Maria Garcia ever since the night of the Spring Thang, and the four of us had been doing stuff together. Mr. Robinson was letting James borrow his car for the prom, it's a black Chrysler LeBaron and we were all definitely looking forward to a trip on those wheels because it almost looked like a small limo and we couldn't afford a real one. We were having dinner at the Space Needle, the prom was at Seattle Center, and then there was an all-night party at the Mt. Baker Community Club so people wouldn't be driving all over the place from party to party getting drunk and crazy. We were going to that party—actually, we had to go there or Mr. Robinson wouldn't lend James the car, and Maria's parents wouldn't let her go to the prom.

Things had been a little tense at James's house the last few weeks. Mona had been asked to the prom by a guy in our class named Nathan Johnson, but since James didn't know him, Mr.

and Mrs. Robinson wouldn't let her go. She had a big fight with her parents about it and she'd been kind of miserable lately whenever I'd been over there. They are pretty strict. Mona confided in me that they would have let her go if the guy had been David or someone they knew, but that she really liked this Nathan guy.

Ever since the Spring Thang I had a special feeling for Mona. We were just friends, but we were close in a nice way. She was the one who made it possible for me to move off the wall. She acted like she felt the same way about me. The Spring Thang had been her first high school dance, and I think my being her brother's friend made me pretty safe.

David never got the nerve to invite anyone, not even someone's sister, so he and some guys he worked with at Kentucky Fried Chicken went to Vancouver, B.C., for the weekend. When people would ask them if they were going to the prom, they'd say they were going to B.C., which made them sound cool—they thought. James and I knew that routine.

I had picked up my tux from the Tux Shop, and was taking the shirt out of the box when Mom stuck her head into my room.

"Look at this." She held up a newspaper. "What is it?" I held the shirt up; it looked kind of wrinkled.

"It's the *Northwest Nikkei,* the Japanese American community paper that comes out each month. Here's Uncle Hideki's picture."

"You're kidding. Let me see." Mom handed me the paper. There he was holding up some calligraphy and standing next to a white guy who held a blue ribbon. The caption under the paper read: "Hideki Suzuyama of Los Angeles, Judge of the Shodo Exhibition, presents First Prize to Michael Haight.

Second and third place winners (not pictured) were Tomi Hiraoka and Michelle Tomura."

"I'm surprised he picked a winner who wasn't Japanese." I looked at the picture.

"The judges have to pick the winners based on the entries, which are only numbered, so they don't know the names of the contestants," Mom explained.

"I bet the old toad croaked when he found out he'd picked a white guy!"

Mom laughed, then she looked at my tux shirt. "This is a little wrinkled."

"I know, I'm going to iron it."

"I'll do it." Mom took the shirt and went into the kitchen.

I followed her. "I don't mind doing it."

Mom got the iron and the ironing board out of the closet. "Believe me, I'll do a better job, you want to look good for Ivy."

"Thanks." I got a Coke and sat at the kitchen table.

"Uncle Hideki looked a lot like my dad in that picture." Mom placed the shirt over the ironing board.

"They sure weren't the same kind of person." I sipped my Coke.

"No, camp seemed to affect them differently. Uncle Hideki got bitter and my dad and mom, I don't know. . . ." Mom stopped ironing for a minute. "They were wonderful with you and Suzanne, but I got all this pressure to do everything right, as if being a model citizen would be a hedge against being thrown in a camp again."

"When are you supposed to get that reparations money?" Mom still had never said anything about it.

"It's distributed to the oldest people first. I don't expect to receive it until the end of this year."

"Maybe you could build a better studio, you've always wanted a bigger one." I took another sip of my Coke.

"I've already thought about it. It's for you kids, but I only want you to use it for education," she said, emphatically. "People can take your home, your car, all your possessions, but no one can ever take away what's inside your head."

Mom started ironing again while I leafed through the newspaper, scanning the headlines. Taiko Theater Ensemble Makes U.S. Debut in Seattle. . .Nihon No Joho (News from Japan). . . Warashibe Kai Holds Golf Tournament at Echo Falls. . .Ayame Kai Rummage Sale to Benefit Seattle Keiro. . . I looked over at Mom.

"You've never been into that much about Japan, have you?" Mom was about to answer when we heard the front door close. Suzanne was home. I heard the rustle of bags. Shopping, no doubt.

"Look at this." I handed Suzanne the paper as she came into the kitchen with a bunch of bags from Nordstrom's Rack.

"What is it?"

"See anyone you know?"

"Oh, there's Uncle Hideous." Suzanne looked at the picture and then sat down with the paper.

"Like I was saying," Mom continued, "Baach and Jiichan put a lot of pressure on me to conform, always worrying about what other people thought of us. I probably rebelled against that by being an artist. Creativity is really the opposite of conformity." She held up the shirt. "What do you think?"

"Looks great, thanks." I hoped Ivy would think so, too.

Mom got a hanger and carefully put the shirt on it. "But it wasn't like I avoided symbols of Japanese culture so I could be more American. I always felt I could never really fit in, not in Japan and not here." She handed me the shirt.

"It's perfect. Mom."

"I've got my camera ready for when you put on your tux." Mom smiled, then she sighed, still stuck on the Hideki thing. "This can be confusing, but it wasn't my Japanese heritage I was trying to get away from. . . it was the pressure to conform that I felt from my parents that I tried to get away from. Maybe that meant being less Japanese, I just don't know."

Suzanne handed Mom the paper. "The thing that got me was how totally rude he was. I couldn't believe it."

"You know, I can't remember being so angry. At least not in a long time. But after that wore off, it was just disappointment." Mom sighed. "I was hoping we'd all like each other." She looked at the paper, studying it. Her eyes filled with sadness and she was quiet for a moment. "It's amazing how much he looks like my dad."

Then she looked away, setting the paper on the table. "It's like he wanted to keep all the traditional things about Japanese culture, but he missed how you should treat people."

"You know that poem you wrote?" I turned to Suzanne.

"Sure, what about it?"

"Could I borrow it?"

"What do you mean borrow it?"

"Use it, I mean, I'd say who wrote it and. . . and everything. I mean, I wouldn't pretend I wrote it."

"Sure, I'll get it for you."

"Thanks. Should I put down, Suzanne Suyama as the author, or that pen name you made up?"

"Put down Suzanne Suyama."

"Thanks." I took the shirt to my room. I wanted to give Ivy a card tonight when I gave her the corsage. I wasn't very good at telling her how I felt about her and all the cards at Pay 'n' Save were either too stupid or too mushy. Suzanne's poem would be perfect.

We got lucky. It was a warm, perfect night. Ivy wore a blue satin dress; she was a total knockout. The corsage was a creamy white gardenia that looked gorgeous against her beautiful skin. I decided to wait to give her the card until later in the evening. It wasn't all that romantic when I gave her the corsage when I picked her up with all her sisters and brothers hanging around and her mom and grandmother taking pictures of us.

After dinner at the Space Needle we all went up to the observation deck. James and Maria strolled over to one corner and Ivy and I went toward the north side, looking over Puget Sound, past Magnolia Bluff, and out toward Whidbey Island. The lights of the ferry boats crossing from Bainbridge Island and Bremerton moved slowly through the twilight. I reached for Ivy and looked into her big dark peanut butter cup eyes.

"Cold?"

"A little."

I took off my tux jacket and put it around her shoulders, first taking the card out of my pocket.

"Suzanne wrote this, but it says how I feel about us," I said, watching Ivy as she opened it.

Cherry trees blossom, crane wings soar
Wind whispers
Autumn fog, the moon of winter

Early spring evolves to summer
Love endures.

"That's beautiful," Ivy smiled.

"I hope that'll happen," I said, "that we'll endure."

"Me, too." Ivy looked up at me and I kissed her and held her close to me for a long time, never wanting to let go.

I didn't know what would happen to Ivy and me — if we would endure. . . but at least we'd have the summer.

ABOUT THE AUTHOR

Jean Davies Okimoto was born in Cleveland, Ohio, and has lived in Michigan, Indiana, Texas, California, and New York; but most of her life has been spent in the Pacific Northwest. She is the co-founder of the Seattle Reading Awards and recipient of many awards including the ALA Best Book for Young Adults Award, the Parent's' Choice Award, the Green Earth Book Award, and is the author of two *Smithsonian* Notable Books. Her debut novel for adults, *The Love Ceiling*, won the 2009 Next Generation ebook Fiction award and was named to the 2010 Indie Next Reading Group List. She and her husband Joe live on Vashon Island near Seattle, Washington. She can be contacted through her website www.jeandaviesokimoto.com.

CPSIA information can be obtained
at www.ICGtesting.com
Printed in the USA
FFOW05n1917230414

9 780982 316795